ALWAYS THE REBEL

Never the Bride
Book 10

Emily E K Murdoch

ARE YOU SIGNED UP FOR DRAGONBLADE'S BLOG?

You'll get the latest news and information on exclusive giveaways, exclusive excerpts, coming releases, sales, free books, cover reveals and more.

Check out our complete list of authors, too!

No spam, no junk. That's a promise!

Sign Up Here

www.dragonbladepublishing.com

Dearest Reader;

Thank you for your support of a small press. At Dragonblade Publishing, we strive to bring you the highest quality Historical Romance from the some of the best authors in the business. Without your support, there is no 'us', so we sincerely hope you adore these stories and find some new favorite authors along the way.

Happy Reading!

CEO, Dragonblade Publishing

Additional Dragonblade books by Author Emily E K Murdoch

Never The Bride Series

Always the Bridesmaid (Book 1)
Always the Chaperone (Book 2)
Always the Courtesan (Book 3)
Always the Best Friend (Book 4)
Always the Wallflower (Book 5)
Always the Bluestocking (Book 6)
Always the Rival (Book 7)
Always the Matchmaker (Book 8)
Always the Widow (Book 9)
Always the Rebel (Book 10)

CHAPTER ONE

SOPHIA TOOK A deep breath and knew there was a high chance she would regret this within five minutes.

Go on, whispered a part of her. *You have nothing left to lose, no pride to protect. They have done everything to you they possibly could. It's time to walk through the world on your own terms.*

A smile flickered across her face as she pushed back a curl of dark hair. The imposing house stood before her, wedding guests staring curiously—or in some cases, in absolute horror.

Her smile broadened. *Well, they were all talking about her anyway, weren't they?* Time to give them something to talk about.

Walking up the steps with far more boldness than she felt, Miss Sophia Worsley entered the wedding reception of the gentleman who, just a few weeks ago, had been her *own* betrothed.

She had never been to Lenskeyn House

before. It was grand, the hallway wide and tall, packed with the few wedding guests who had deigned to attend Jacob Beauvale's scandalous wedding.

Not for much longer. As Sophia stood in the doorway with a bright smile, every eye turned from their conversations, the champagne handed out by liveried footmen, the bride and groom— and toward her.

The whispering started immediately. Sophia's smile did not falter as her quivering fingers smoothed down the linen of the breeches she had chosen for the occasion.

It was bold. After all, their footman, Alexander, would not notice his spare breeches were missing until it was all over, and she was almost sure she could return them without him guessing.

Although now that she looked at everyone from Bath's highest society, she wondered whether the rumors would reach the footman before the breeches did.

Sophia took a few steps forward and helped herself to a flute of champagne from a footman unable to speak. A garbled groan emerged from his mouth, and Sophia winked.

"What a wonderful wedding reception," she said to him in a mock whisper, ignoring the scandalized murmurs shifting around the room. "This should have been mine, you know."

The poor footman, only about fifteen years

of age, had not expected a young lady to arrive at the wedding reception wearing tight breeches and a gentleman's shirt.

Sophia grinned and stepped away, inclining her head to Lady Romeril, who was turning an interesting shade of beetroot. She could almost hear the woman's unspoken retort.

"Miss Sophia Worsley—and in breeches, too! It is disgraceful, the very idea! Everyone can see her ankles—her calves! And the way it—no, it is simply not to be borne. After everything I have done for her!"

Sophia passed Lady Romeril without saying a word. Forgiveness would come, but she was not quite ready to speak with Lady Romeril. Not after she had orchestrated Sophia's most significant embarrassment to date.

No, she was done with gentlemen, done with marriage. The entire affair had taught her one thing: *men were not to be trusted, and if she was going to be happy, it would be alone.*

A voice rose above the chatter. *The bride.* The woman who had stolen her fiancée on the very day of her wedding and was now married to Jacob. Elizabeth was laughing at a joke, nothing but love on their faces.

It was enough to make Sophia sick.

"You know, I can never say my life has been dull," the new Mrs. Beauvale was saying to Jacob with a mischievous smile. "Why, for a moment there in the church when I saw…"

Her gaze had been moving about the room, taking in the splendor of her wedding reception, but halted abruptly when it fell on Sophia. Jacob turned around, and his mouth fell open.

Sophia's smile did not disappear. There was no warmth in her eyes. Jacob did not deserve warmth. No, what he deserved was unspeakable. But his jilted fiancée appearing at his wedding reception in breeches?

That was a start.

Sophia bowed as more guests started to notice. Their gasps were becoming quite audible, but not enough to mask the astonishing comments.

"Is that a lady in breeches?"

"Good God, what will they think of next?"

"She looks remarkably familiar—Christ, is that Miss Worsley? The first bride?"

And amongst them all, Sophia was able to make out the cutting remarks of the woman who had seduced her intended and convinced him to leave her at the altar.

"Well," breathed Elizabeth with a laugh, "that is bold."

"She cannot be serious," Jacob said quietly. "What does she think she's playing at?"

This was intolerable. Heat rose in Sophia's chest and up her neck, but she would not permit them to control this situation. She was the rebel here, and she would have her way.

"Good afternoon, all, and what a lovely day it has been," said Sophia loudly, her voice carrying. "Though what you are all looking at, I cannot imagine. Is there any punch anywhere, do you know?"

For the shortest of moments, her gaze caught Jacob's. His eyes did not waver. It could all have been so different if only he had been loyal. If only he had been brave enough to ignore the woman attempting to get her claws into him.

This would have been her wedding reception. *It would all have been so different.*

"Jacob," Sophia said, against her will. She had promised herself she would not attempt to speak with him, but there he was, just feet away, and—

Without saying a word, he turned away. He took his new wife's hand and strode on, slamming the door behind them.

Silence now rang out in the hall. Faces turned to look at her, and there was no kindness, no commiseration as she deserved. No, pure judgment rained down silently, and Sophia stood, head held high, against them all.

How dare they. It was outrageous—it was criminal! If she had a brother, he would have called out Jacob for abandoning her after a year's engagement.

He had promised to marry her. He had proposed, and he had met her parents. Her father had grown to like him. And now he was in another room, undoubtedly kissing the woman he had been slighting her for the entire time. *It had all been a lie.*

The whispering started again. Sophia knew precisely what they were saying as she sipped her cold champagne, the bubbles making her feel a little more alive.

Yes, that was the Worsley girl, poor thing. Jilted at the altar, and at almost three and twenty. She was fast running out of time, and how would she find a gentleman to marry her wearing breeches in public!

Sophia's eyes narrowed. *Well, she would never marry now.* Gentlemen simply were not worth the agonizing over. And if turning up in breeches brought a little notoriety to the happy couple, they deserved it.

"That was poorly done, my girl, and I think you will regret it."

Sophia turned around with a sickly smile for Lady Romeril. "Good afternoon to you, too, Lady Romeril."

The elderly lady ignored the sycophantic tone. "No need to tie yourself up in knots, Miss Worsley. You should not have come, and you know that."

Late into her seventies, Lady Romeril was a bastion of polite society. *She should never have permitted the older woman to introduce her to Jacob.* That was where it had all started, when her life had fallen apart.

"Why not?" Sophia said lightly, finishing her glass of champagne. "All of Jacob's family and acquaintances are here, and I know him almost as well as anyone."

The words came from a long way off, but Sophia forced down the pain that would, in time, cause tears to fall.

Lady Romeril was shaking her head. "I know it was a shock—"

"A shock!" Sophia did not bother to keep her voice down. *Why should she?* The bride and groom had not rejoined their wedding celebration. God knew what they were doing, so she would provide the guests with entertainment. "A shock? After waiting for a full twelvemonth? Then he decides midway through our vows before God to walk away from me?"

Each word jabbed another dart into her heart. *The—the damned man! How could he have treated her like that?* After she had been so vulnerable, and after he knew what had happened before?

"The way I heard it," Lady Romeril said low with a stern look, "you attempted to blackmail my godson into carrying out his commitment to you. Hardly a ladylike endeavor."

Sophia swallowed. The pointed glares from the other wedding guests were starting to irritate her, but she could not stop them. Her mere presence was enough, but the breeches were gaining true attention.

A prickle of regret attempted to sear her heart, but she pushed the emotion away. She was going to see this through.

"True, I did attempt to reason with his better nature," she said quietly. "But only after...he was the one seeing her the whole time!"

"And if I had known, I would certainly have advised him to choose between you two much earlier," said Lady Romeril with a sniff. "What a fool he was—but a fool, not a brigand."

"I think you may have felt differently," said Sophia haughtily, "if it was your daughter, or you, Lady Romeril, who had been jilted at the altar. And besides..."

She coughed and wondered whether she was bold enough to say it. But this was Lady Romeril, after all. *She undoubtedly knew.*

"I have been jilted before, as I am sure you know," she said, her voice lowering for the first time in their conversation. "*He* knew it. I told him...told him not to break my heart."

The last word wavered, and the fierce sting of tears threatened in her eyes.

This was a mistake. She should not have come to the wedding, let alone the reception. But she had to see it—she had to see him married. Otherwise, she would always wonder, a small part of her would always hope.

All her hopes had come to naught. It was

galling to see him married to another, painful to see Mrs. Howard become Mrs. Beauvale—*her name*. The name she should have had.

And the child, too. Yes, everyone said that the widowed Howard's child was her first husband's, but Sophia was not so sure. No matter what Jacob told the world, that baby was his.

It was rather rebellious of him, really, and she had never thought he had it in him. Bedding a woman and getting her with child mere weeks before her husband died.

A carriage accident. Sophia snorted. *No one believed that.*

Lady Romeril was evidently expecting her to speak.

Sophia sighed. "I may have been wrong to attempt to force the engagement through to a wedding, but I had to take things into my own hands."

The older woman raised her eyebrows. "How original."

A flicker of irritation soared through Sophia's mind. "I have no brothers, and you have met my father. Who else did you think was going to stand for my rights as an engaged woman?"

Lady Romeril nodded. "You felt as though you had no one to speak for you?"

Sophia opened her mouth to reply but was distracted. The door had opened, and the bride and groom, beaming and both looking a little pink in the face, entered the hallway to cheers from their guests.

She shook her head. "No one to speak for me, no one to act for me. No one to do the right thing by me, and so yes, I attempted to force the issue. It did not work, of course."

No matter the pain, she could not look away. Jacob's smile was broad, his forehead untroubled. His hand was around the waist of his bride as she laughed at something he said.

They were so happy. So unbearably happy.

"And here I am, unmarried after two engagements," said Sophia bitterly. "No gentleman will ever wish to marry me now."

"Not in those breeches, at any rate," snapped Lady Romeril. "Get a grip of yourself, Miss Worsley. Go home before you embarrass yourself any further."

With a sweep of silks, she was gone.

Sophia held her head up high despite her instinct to leave, hail her carriage, and go straight home for a good cry. She had been determined to come here and show the world how little she cared that Jacob had married his new bride.

It had not worked. They were as happy as ever.

Sophia's gaze moved around the room. The few people she recognized glared. There was Mrs. Lymington and Mrs. Marnion. They had been talking quietly together, but as Sophia looked at them, they both ceased talking and then spoke more rapidly.

Sophia swallowed. *She did not care.* Mrs. Marnion was a tittle-tattle gossip, and Mrs. Lymington was far too high and mighty. Her husband's wealth from trade may have given her daughters large dowries but had bought them no elegance.

Continuing to look around the room, she saw Mrs. Cheswick. Sophia smiled. She had known her daughter, Tabitha, for years. Mrs. Cheswick frowned and looked meaningfully away. Sophia's smile faded. That had been before Tabitha had married the Duke of Axwick, of course. Now Mrs. Cheswick's grandson would be a duke.

Taking deep strides across the room—something which would have been impossible in a gown—Sophia poked her head into a side room where gentlemen were playing cards.

It had been full of good-natured chatter and boisterous laughter, but the room fell silent as she stood in the doorway, cigar smoke wafting up to the ceiling.

A nervous laugh erupted in one corner, and then chatter rose into the awkward silence. Sophia took a brave step forward.

Perhaps it was the breeches. Gentlemen always seemed to know what they were doing. *No wonder gentlemen liked to wear them. They had a certain power skirts lacked.*

Moving to the nearest table with an empty seat, Sophia lowered herself and smiled at the inhabitants of the card game.

"Deal me in," she said sweetly.

Abraham Fitzclarence, Viscount Braedon, gave one of his characteristic chuckles.

"Miss Worsley, how delightful to see you! But you have to know I cannot possibly allow you to—"

Sophia had had enough. The champagne had utterly gone to her head—at least, the bubbles had—and she was tired of being laughed at. And at the same time, she gloried in it. It made no sense. She could not understand herself, but cards, she knew.

"Deal me in," she said firmly, "if you know what is good for you, Braedon."

The Duke of Axwick was seated beside him and laughed along with a gentleman she did not recognize.

"You have a wild one there, Braedon," said the unknown gentleman who had blond hair and a teasing air. "Don't tell me she is one of yours?"

"Behave yourself, Larnwick, and meet Miss Sophia Worsley," Braedon said irritably, dealing out the cards. "Miss Worsley, Colin Vaughn, Duke of Larnwick."

Sophia inclined her head but did not allow it to be turned. A duke, an earl, a viscount—those titles had mattered when she had been on the marriage market, hunting for a husband.

No longer. Gentlemen were just people, usually inferior, and not to be tolerated.

She looked down at her cards. Unlike most young ladies, her father had taught her card games, including poker for something to do in long winter evenings, and she had gained quite a knack at bluffing. But a poker player was only as good as the hand they were dealt.

This was a very good hand.

"What is our blind?" she said as casually as she could.

The Duke of Larnwick laughed again. "Goodness, I like your style, Miss Worsley. A shilling, but here, let me."

He placed two shillings into the center of the table, along with a small pile of silver before her.

The Sophia from a few years ago would have blushed, dissembled, hoping to speak with him later. *She had grown up since then.* She nodded and concentrated on her cards.

Easier said than done. Out of the corner of her eyes, she could see gentlemen from other tables standing up to have a good look.

Bad news travels fast.

"Two kings on the table, with a four, an eight, and a two," said Braedon, their dealer. "Let the ridiculous bluffing commence!"

Every face in the room was turned to her, save one. Sophia found herself unconsciously drawn to the gentleman who was ignoring her.

She could see little of him from here. Well dressed, by the look of his coat. Handsome probably, by the line of his jaw. But other than that, he was only remarkable because of his utter disinterest in her.

Sophia shook her head. Every time she thought she had moved past the desire to be noticed by gentlemen, she had to go and find herself intrigued by another one.

"Aha!" the Duke of Axwick said with a grin. "There, three of a kind."

"Three eights, my word," said the Duke of Larnwick. "Beats anything I have."

Braedon was shaking his head sadly. "Me, too. Well done, gentlemen—oh, Miss Worsley."

His eyes grew wide as Sophia laid down her three kings. "I should have bet a little higher."

There were astonished laughs around the table, and a few gentlemen from the other side of the room stood up to see what was going on now.

Sophia found a sudden rush of joy move through her. *There was something so pleasing about winning a hand of cards.*

Braedon laughed. "More gentleman than lady, I think, you rebel!"

Sophia smiled. After all that had occurred to her, perhaps that was all she could be now. *A lady without a gentleman. Without any desire for one.*

A true rebel.

CHAPTER TWO

I T WAS RARE Philip Egerton, Earl of Marnmouth, ever regretted anything but this evening was one of those times.

Christ in his Heaven, what had he been thinking when he had invited this rabble to his table?

Perhaps he was getting too old for all this nonsense. Even Axwick was younger than him, and Marnmouth had found himself in bed before nine o'clock last night!

This was it. The end of times.

"Surely not!" guffawed Colin Vaughn, Duke of Larnwick. "I cannot believe you!"

Marnmouth smiled mechanically. A Saturday evening, only weeks before the Season began, and here he was at his table, bored out of his mind. Nothing better to do but to invite his acquaintances to dine, and still, he was bored.

There had once been a time when he would not have known which invitation to accept for a

Saturday night's entertainment. Cards, gambling, dances, shoots in the morning, and billiards in the evenings.

"Port and cheese, my lord," said McCall, his butler, as the footmen brought it through.

Marnmouth nodded. McCall had run the Marnmouth houses for years. More timely than clockwork, more dependable than any mechanism, he removed any responsibility from his master's shoulders.

God's teeth, another course. Port and cheese. If he was not so well-mannered, he would rise from this table and walk away.

And it was his dinner!

With every year, the more tiresome the world became. *Had it always been this uninteresting, or had he simply not noticed until now?*

"—and that was when he realized the wench was his daughter!" Braedon crowed, finishing his tale.

They all laughed, Richard St. Maur, the Duke of Axwick, having to wipe tears from his eyes. "Braedon, I cannot believe the poor man did not recognize her!"

"Why not?" Chester shot back, nodding at the butler pouring port into his glass. "The man simply does not pay attention. You know that. Everyone knows it!"

More laughter as they helped themselves to the very best port in London. All except Axwick.

He placed his hand over his glass as the butler came around, and when the servant looked questioningly at his master, Marnmouth nodded. The Duke of Axwick did not imbibe.

Which was a shame, for it was marvelously good stuff. He had spent an excessive amount of time questioning his cellarer back at Marnmouth Heights, and was assured it was the finest that could be procured.

He did not ask precisely how. His seat on the cliffs of Devon was perfectly riddled with caves, clever little ports, and landings for ships coming in from France. *It was best one did not know.*

"I have to commend you, Marnmouth."

He blinked and saw Braedon was smiling. "You do?"

The viscount nodded. "This port—I do not believe I have tasted finer all year. You are to be congratulated. I do not know how you do it."

The man winked and laughed along with his fellow guests, and Marnmouth smiled mechanically.

Braedon was a good sort. Not to everyone's tastes, a little rowdy for some, and at times he spoke without considering a single syllable. They had…well, not exactly come to *blows* in the past. Nothing so sordid as that. But Braedon had certainly embarrassed himself at Marnmouth's table before, and it was clear he was not the only one recalling this.

"Yes, very fine," said Chester hastily. "But then, much like the rest of your table. If you ever find yourself looking for a replacement cook, Marnmouth, I would be happy to take yours off your hands!"

The suggestion of smuggling passed by, and Marnmouth nodded at Chester in silent acknowledgment. *It did not do to even suggest such a thing.*

Poor Braedon. Not the sharpest tool in the box, thought Marnmouth. He liked him as a rule, but the younger gentleman was more often well-intentioned than well-spoken.

"And now I have congratulations to give," said Axwick, picking at the cheese selection he had placed on his plate. "To Larnwick, the gentleman who has managed to remain single for the longest time I could imagine with a bride waiting in the wings!"

Laughter rang out across the table as glasses were raised, and toasts were drunk. Marnmouth raised his automatically but did not drink. Larnwick was a close friend of Axwick, he knew, but he was not personally acquainted with the details of this supposed match.

"Aye, ye can laugh y'selves silly if you wish," said Larnwick, his native Scots coming through as he downed another glass of port. "But it cannae last long. No, my wedding fast approaches quicker than I can run from it!"

The conversation continued around the table, but Marnmouth had little interest in it. He had never delved into the matrimonial plans of others, more interested in ensuring McCall brought out his favorite cigars.

"So, how is your Miss Lymington?" said Axwick with a grin. "I have seen her of course, 'tis difficult to miss her."

"Only because there are so many of them," Chester laughed. "Is it four daughters? I never seem to attend anything without the twins there—and I apologize in advance, Larnwick, but I cannot tell them apart and have no comprehension, which will become your wife!"

"As if it matters!" Braedon cut in.

Marnmouth frowned. *Someone needed to take Braedon in hand if he was going to stay in the best society.*

"After all, there are far more of us single gentlemen here than marrieds," said Braedon, his eyes bright. "Axwick and Chester are the minority here, so let's not dwell on the ladies too much."

"Ah yes, but the balance of power may shift quicker than you think if you believe the rumors," said Axwick with a grin at his host. "Surely our host will join us before too long."

All eyes shifted to Marnmouth. The room was starting to fill up with the sweet oaky smell of his favorite cigars, and he smiled as he held court in the silence.

He should have expected this. The moment he had put Emma Tilbury aside and taken no other mistress, the rumors had started. *Who was Philip Egerton, Earl of Marnmouth, to marry now that his mistress of several years had been abandoned?*

"I am not seeking a wife," he said calmly, "but if one came along and presented herself…"

He allowed his voice to fade away, often the quickest way to end this particular line of questioning.

"I suppose Miss Tilbury has already presented herself and been declined?" Braedon asked.

No one smiled. The room became silent as Braedon quickly realized he had, once again, overstepped the mark.

"Damnit, man, one topic to avoid, and you don't manage it," Marnmouth heard Chester whisper to his friend.

Marnmouth smiled. One did not take a mistress for years, cover her in diamonds, flaunt her at Almack's, and then decide to…discontinue the entanglement without attracting a little gossip, he knew that.

But damn it, it had been—what, two years now? He thought the gossips would have found something more interesting, but Braedon did have some sort of bizarre interest in her.

"You know, I have heard it all about my previous mistress, Emma Tilbury," he said delicately, "and so nothing you have to say will surprise me. You think I do not understand what she wanted? But marriage was not in my power to offer her, and so we parted ways."

"You do not have to speak any further," said Axwick gruffly.

Marnmouth saw the duke's discomfort but shrugged. "I keep no secrets. In fact, I believe myself to be remarkably open about my dealings with the ladies. I think you all, save Larnwick, were at that dinner a few years ago when I said just how a mistress could not satisfy as a wife could. So, no secrets."

Braedon's gaze had dropped to his hands folded in his lap, and a tinge of red seared Axwick's cheeks. Marnmouth had to remind himself that, though a duke, Axwick had never taken a mistress, never gambled, never taken a drink. *Not after his family history.*

Larnwick, the gentleman he knew the least, was looking round the room as though desperate for a change in conversation.

It was Chester who broke the silence. "I remember that dinner most precisely. I think overdue thanks are in order, Marnmouth. It was your words that convinced me to go and get my wife out of the hole she had been placed in."

He took a slightly too large swig of the port and coughed. Marnmouth found himself, for the first time that evening, stirred from his stupor.

Chester's words intrigued him.

He had heard the gossip, of course. *Who had not?* The gossip rags had been full of the tittle-tattle when the sister of the Duke of Mercia had gone missing, and they had had a field day when she had been found, years later, in a brothel.

The fact it had been Chester to have found her, unknowing she was a gentlelady and the sister of his acquaintance…

Well. Marnmouth had paid a good deal of money for the full story from the footman who had seen the fight firsthand, good manners preventing him from asking Chester directly.

How exactly did one ask how a fellow's wife had become a courtesan?

As though the man could hear his thoughts, Chester grinned. "Yes, plenty of people have been desperate to ask, and I have no concern with sharing the truth as long as it is then recounted in full—but if I am honest, there is no great dramatic story."

Larnwick leaned forward. "I do not believe I have heard of it. How you encountered your wife, I presume?"

Marnmouth opened his mouth to speak. *He would not permit his guest to dig himself that deep a hole by complete chance.*

But Chester was unperturbed. "You have been outside polite society for a good time, Larnwick, if whispers never reached you! Yes, I came across her in not entirely illustrious circumstances, but as soon as I realized who she was, I made her an offer and after almost fighting with her brother—"

"*Almost* fighting?" interrupted Braedon, his boyish charm and thoughtlessness returning. The glasses of port were almost empty now. "I heard it was fisticuffs!"

Marnmouth nodded at a footman who moved forward and refilled his guests' glasses.

"This all sounds rather more like a novel," said Larnwick with a smile. Marnmouth could see his newest acquaintance was not entirely sure whether to believe the tall tale.

Chester nodded. "It was rather, but we are happy now."

Marnmouth smiled. *Time to tie off this conversation.* "I must admit myself a little surprised that my words created such a happily ever after, but I am pleased."

"The only happily ever after you've created, Marnmouth," said Braedon with a wild look in his eyes. "Poor old Emma, I think she hoped it would be hers!"

The table fell silent once again, until—

"Braedon?" said Axwick pleasantly. "Shut up."

The entire table laughed, including Marnmouth. *Well, he was hardly a man to hold a grudge, and it was clear that port had loosened Braedon's tongue.*

Besides, he was a good deal older than the boy. Older than anyone else at this table. At one and forty, nothing could surprise him. At least Braedon said what he was thinking—what most people in society were thinking if they were honest.

The conversation drifted toward more companionable and polite topics, and Marnmouth found himself a disinterested observer rather than a participant.

Dull, dull, dull. A small spark of interest, maybe for five minutes, and then back to the minutiae of life that simply could not hold his interest.

It was an hour later, according to the chiming grandfather clock in the corner, that his guests started to depart.

"No, I simply cannot have another cigar," said Axwick with a grin. "The last thing I want to do is develop a bad habit—no, I mean it, Marnmouth. Your hospitality is legendary as ever—good night to you."

Marnmouth clasped his hand in the hallway of his London residence and then turned to the last of his guests, who had just had his greatcoat pulled on by McCall.

"I cannot thank you enough for being included in this evening," said Larnwick.

Marnmouth nodded. *He did not see the reason for this overindulgent gratitude—he was a mere earl, and Larnwick was a duke, albeit a Scottish title.*

"My pleasure," he said aloud. "And I shall be sure to include you in future goings-on, won't I, McCall?"

He grinned as his elderly butler nodded stiffly. "Consider yourself to have an open invitation, Your Grace."

Larnwick beamed. "My word, thank you. Good evening, Marnmouth."

Marnmouth watched from his doorway as Larnwick unsteadily pulled himself into his carriage before it trundled away—revealing a figure in a gown, fur around her shoulders.

Marnmouth groaned. *Of course. It could not be supposed he could endure even one day without...*

Miss Emma Tilbury stepped into the light. "Have you missed me?"

He sighed. Time and time again, they had danced around this conversation, and lately, he had been a little harsh to ensure she had understood.

And yet, here she was. Again.

In the full knowledge his words would only cause her pain, he took a deep breath. He would never lie to her. *She had earned the truth.*

"No, I have not missed you," he said baldly.

Emma stepped closer. "If you just give me a few minutes, I am sure I can convince you."

The smallest hint of desire flickered in his heart, but Marnmouth pushed it aside. He had promised he would never toy with her.

"No, Emma, you are not coming in," he said calmly.

There was movement behind him, and he saw from the corner of his eye that his butler had left them alone. *Good. McCall always knew what was expected of him.*

Emma was pouting as she moved up the steps to stand before him. Marnmouth swallowed and tasted the desire on his lips.

Blast it, he was human, after all.

"We have parted ways," Marnmouth said in his most decisive voice. "I have never lied to you, Emma. We are nothing to each other."

Now she had stepped into the light, he could see what he had not noticed in the murky darkness of the evening. Emma Tilbury was still just as beautiful as when she had first caught his eye, but was now a little rough around the edges. Her gown needed to be rehemmed, and her jewelry no longer sparkled like the diamonds he had given her in their heady days.

A trip to the pawnbrokers, he realized, guilt pouring into his bones. *Well, he had done what he could when she had been his, and there was nothing he could do now.*

Besides, when they had parted, she had taken away with her more than a fair sum. Huge. A dowry intended to help her find a husband. But instead…

"Poor Philip," Emma crooned, leaning against the doorway in that damned suggestive way she knew he liked. "You look tired, you poor man. You can say you do not miss me as much as you like, but I can see you need a little...companionship."

Marnmouth's jaw tightened. "No, I have just had some friends for dinner."

Emma grinned. "Female companionship."

Attempting to ignore the way her waist curved so delightfully to her bottom, Marnmouth said, "I know you better than anyone."

She nodded, leaning closer.

He took a step back. "And so you should know I speak the truth when I say I am not interested. Bored with life I may be, but I am not going to return to bad habits."

It was poor phrasing, he knew that as soon as the words were out of his mouth. A frown appeared between Emma's eyes, and she straightened up.

"I am not merely a habit!" she said with more feeling in her words. "I am a person!"

"Nevertheless," said Marnmouth, "I am not interested."

She examined him, and then her smile returned. "You jest. Come on, Philip, you have never restrained yourself from what you enjoy before."

Emma reached out a hand, and he took it—

but only to force her backward.

"Emma, I have been kind, I have been patient, I have been firm, and I have never wavered in my decision," he said quietly. The last thing he wanted was for one of his neighbors to see what appeared to be an assignation. "The only woman who will tempt me is one who truly surprises me."

She laughed at that. "Surprise you? Philip, darling, be serious. You have seen everything— *enjoyed* everything from me. A woman who surprises you? Impossible."

Marnmouth shrugged. *Time to end this pointless debate.* "So be it. My point is, you need to forget me and move on. Go and find another protector, a husband." He did not mention the dowry. *That had evidently been spent months ago.* "I am sure there are plenty of others who will happily extend their honor to you."

For the first time in their conversation, Emma looked unsure whether she understood. Her face had fallen, the tiredness she had been keeping at bay seeping through.

"You would think so, wouldn't you?"

It was not possible to have known her for so long and not feel pity. Marnmouth felt inside his waistcoat and pulled out his pocketbook. There was a five-pound note in it, and this was what he held out for her.

Emma pushed his hand away. "Money? I do

not want your charity, Philip. I want to be your mistress!"

There was a hint of desperation in there that pained him, but he had to say, "I am not in the market for a mistress."

The woman who had once been closer to him than any other arched an eyebrow. "If you are in the market for a wife, I can also consider that."

Marnmouth laughed despite himself. Emma had always been very witty, very clever with her words. *It was one of the reasons he had kept her as a mistress for so long.*

"Give up, Emma," he said gently. "Take my carriage to where you are staying, and then leave me be. Until I find a woman to surprise me, there will be no Countess of Marnmouth."

CHAPTER THREE

S OPHIA LEANED BACK in the rapidly moving carriage and wondered, not for the first time, whether she had made another huge mistake.

As if the wedding reception had not been enough! When she had finally returned home after an excruciating two hours at Lenskeyn House, she had ignored her parents' questions shouted from the drawing room and rushed upstairs to replace the breeches she had...*stolen* was a strong word. *Borrowed.*

Now she was about to do something even more scandalous. *What had possessed her to even think of such a thing?*

As the carriage jolted to a halt, Sophia thought bitterly of the conversation at that morning's breakfast table that had prompted this whole foolish affair.

"And of course, even though your mother and I will be unable to accompany you, you will behave—you *will* behave, won't you, Sophia?" Her father had looked stern over his cup of tea, and Sophia had hated being treated like a child.

"Naturally, she will," her mother had said calmly. "Our little Sophia never does anything without our approval, do you, dear?"

And that had been it. When Sophia, no longer two or even twelve, but almost three and twenty, had stomped up the stairs, she had vowed she absolutely would not behave herself at Almack's that evening.

Peering out of her carriage window, she saw countless ladies stepping down from their carriages, plumes of feathers in their hair and diamonds around their necks. Beautiful gowns of the latest style were illuminated by the fiery torches around Almack's as footmen bowed in the latest guests.

Sophia swallowed. *How long had it been since she was last here?* She had not been engaged then, though there had been murmurings some of society's most elegant and eligible gentlemen were going to be in Bath that Season.

Perhaps a year? Maybe a little longer. Of course, her voucher was still accepted—Lady Romeril had seen to that. Sophia shook her head with a wry smile. *At least the older woman's guilt could be put to some sort of use.*

The Worsleys had lived in Bath for almost an entire year, and so had missed Almack's—but of course, it had all been for the best reason. Jacob Beauvale lived in Bath, had done for years, and so the easiest way to plan the wedding was to stay in Bath.

What a fool she had been. Sophia shook her head as though ridding water from her ears. This was not an evening to think of the gentleman who had taken her heart and so rudely stomped on it. Not another thought of Jacob Beauvale…*no, she would not even consider his name. This evening was to enjoy herself.*

As Sophia looked nervously down at the outfit she had carefully chosen for such an event, she smiled. Her heart had always been free, and that was how she was going to act. She wanted to leave behind the pain and have a little fun.

"You all right, Miss Worsley?"

"Yes, thank you. Almost ready."

Sophia took a deep breath. True, Jacob had hurt her and embarrassed her, pained her, made her more furious than she thought possible. But truly injured her? No, his charms had not touched her heart. Nor had Robert, even when he had been professing words of love.

She had never loved either of them. Security, protection, respect, a good income: those were all things she had sought in a suitor. After all, her father was not going to live forever, despite her mother's insistence.

When she had first entered society, she had

done precisely what had been expected of her. She had sought a husband. Now, she was not so sure. *Perhaps instead of finding a gentleman to care for her, she could just look after herself.*

A knock on the carriage roof. "You sure y'are quite well, Miss Worsley?"

Sophia found her voice. "Yes, I am just…adjusting my hair. One moment, please!"

Hairpins, jewelry, all the baubles society expected her to wear. She did so because it pleased her mother, but she saw little point in them.

Besides, that was not what everyone would look at. She had decided to steal—*borrow* the butler's breeches this time. Alexander was a slip of a thing, and even she had been a little shocked at how tight his breeches had been on her legs.

But their butler was an older gentleman, a little broader. His breeches still fitted her but left more to the imagination.

Not much more. Sophia swallowed. Was this rebellious streak soaring through her heart starting to go too far? Or was this the right amount to show the world she simply did not care about their rules and regulations?

Why should a lady not wear breeches? They were far more practical, and Sophia had made a mental note to attempt horseback riding in breeches in a normal saddle. *Sidesaddle was so tiresome.*

Besides, she was hardly on the hunt for a husband. Gentlemen could go hang, for all she cared. Better to rebel and be her own person than one of those simpering fools she saw trotting up into Almack's desperate to find someone to marry.

Marry? Miss Sophia Worsley would never marry, not now. She had seen too much of the gentlemen around town to believe they had any sense whatsoever. She was tired of their nonsense, lies, their simpering flattery that led nowhere. The question was, was she brave enough to step out of the carriage?

Before she could answer, the carriage door was flung open, and her irate driver appeared in the gleaming light of Almack's.

"Really, miss, I have been waiting for… Christ almighty."

Sophia considered this a sign it was time to disembark. "Out of my way, please."

She had the presence of mind to grab her reticule as she stepped out of the carriage, her cheeks heating as the driver's face turned purple.

"Thank you," she said hastily and turned to march into Almack's—walking headfirst into another person.

"Oh, I am sorry, sir, I was not—Miss Worsley?" Miss Olivia Lymington was staring in abject horror, her gaze taking in her tight white breeches.

Sophia grinned. "Hallo."

If anything, this pronouncement increased rather than reassured the shock on Miss Lymington's face.

"What on earth happened to—you are wearing breeches!"

Sophia nodded. *Really, it was worth it, even if she did not step a foot into Almack's, to see one of the Lymington girls speechless.*

"I know, and far more comfortable, too," she said conversationally. "I cannot believe I have not made the change sooner. As soon as I have attempted riding a horse, I will inform you whether or not 'tis much easier, as I suppose. I highly recommend them to anyone who wants to get anything done."

Without waiting for Miss Lymington to answer, Sophia turned on her heels and started up the steps to Almack's.

Well, if that was just a snippet of what she could expect for the rest of the evening, it was going to be an entertaining one.

How had she never noticed how frustrating it was to take small mincing steps in a gown? She got so much further, so much quicker, when in breeches. Her confident steps belied the panic surging in her heart. If that was the response of a lady who knew her, what on earth would be the reactions of the great and the good in there?

But despite it all, Sophia found herself smiling. A small part of her…well, *liked it*. Enjoyed the stares, reveled in the whispering. It was pleasant in a strange way, to be stared at and gossiped about for something she had chosen herself. Better they gawp, for gawp they would, due to her rebellious clothing than because another gentleman had left her at the altar.

At the top of the steps, it was evident by the panicked look on the footman's face he was seriously considering barring her entry.

Sophia did not give him time to consider it. Smiling sweetly, she tilted her hips slightly in that way she knew would set him aflutter. "Is there anything wrong, kind sir?"

The poor man was only human, she thought as he turned red and started to splutter, words getting lost between tongue and lips as his eyes were drawn to her buttocks.

"N-no p-p-problem, m-miss," he said, voice squeaking and head shaking.

Sophia kissed him on the cheek, to scandalized gasps. "Thank you."

The inner hallway was silent as faces turned to see what whippersnapper had turned up in such breeches.

Sophia stood tall, meeting the eye of everyone who turned to stare, and at that moment, she knew she could glory in this attention for the rest of her life.

She was going to be the talk of society by the

end of the night, and probably for the first time in her life, it was going to be about something of her choosing, her own decision—not that someone else has decided not to marry her.

Inclining her head politely to those she passed, Sophia walked through the inner hallway and towards the greater room where the noise of dancing was emanating.

The dancing did not precisely stop as she stepped through the doorway, but there were fumbled footsteps and muttering as people stared.

Sophia's smile widened. *Was this how it felt to be notorious? Why had she waited this long to do something a little different?*

"Sophia Worsley, as I live and breathe!"

She turned to see who had called her name, and her defiant smile softened as she saw Harry. One of her oldest and most loyal friends, even when separated by her time on the Continent, she had rallied behind her after both jiltings and was now striding across Almack's.

She left a group, including her husband, Monty, and a few gentlemen she did not know.

"What on earth possessed you to wear them?" Harry said by way of greeting as she took Sophia's hands in her own.

Sophia shrugged. "Why on earth not?"

Laughing, Harry said, "Well, you must see the reactions of those around us—I am sure if Braedon was here, he would hardly be able to keep his eyes in his head!"

Sophia said fiercely, "I do not see any reason why a lady cannot wear something more comfortable than a gown, even to Almack's."

Her friend dropped her hands but continued to smile, bringing Sophia some well-needed relief. *There was no point in being rebellious if it lost one's friends.*

Even Harry, or Harriet, as her mother called her, was a rebel in her own way, but as a duchess, it would have been easy to shun her friend, arriving at Almack's in such a fashion.

"And I thought I was rebellious for refusing to lose my childhood nickname," said Harry with a grin. "You fool, Sophia. You think your parents won't hear about this?"

Relief spread across Sophia's heart. "You have never rebelled in your life?"

A strange look passed over her friend's face, and Harry, unusually, blushed. "One day, I will tell you how I managed to seduce Monty and make him marry me. Then, perhaps, you will believe I am the rebellious one of the two of us."

They were words designed to intrigue. Sophia had never heard the full tale of how Harry and Monty had suddenly found themselves man and wife.

Opening her mouth to ask, Sophia was immediately halted by Harry.

"Not today," she said, raising a gloved hand.

"Not now. But come and stand with us. You will not find anyone else willing to stand with you in that get-up. Come on."

Sophia looked away from her friend and saw space on all sides. People had been moving away, wild and reckless as she evidently was, and one matron tugged her daughter aside and whispered something meant to chastise.

She laughed. "So I can see. Who is with you this evening?"

They started walking as Harry replied, "One of them you already know."

She did indeed. As the two ladies reached Harry's group, Braedon grinned. "My word, Miss Worsley, you certainly know how to make an entrance! Is that really you?"

"Really," Sophia said with a wry smile, "and why you gentlemen have been keeping the secret of how comfortable breeches are for so long, I will never know!"

"Perhaps because they knew how delectable you would look in them and did not want to cause a riot," said a stranger's voice.

While Braedon, Harry, and Monty chuckled at her joke, Sophia colored and turned to see who had approached her.

He was tall, handsome, and she thought she knew him. She met his eyes, and her skin warmed at the intensity of his look.

He was the gentleman at Jacob's wedding

reception who had not looked at her. Older than her, but with all the attractiveness that maturity and wisdom of years brought, there was a little silver around his temples and a knowing smile on his lips.

It was startling how intense her physical reaction to him was. Jacob had never done this to her. *No man ever had.*

"Riot?" she said as calmly as she could. "I would hardly think my legs could cause a riot."

The gentleman had not bothered to introduce himself, so Sophia could not chastise him by name as his gaze moved slowly down her, taking in every inch of her body now on display thanks to her stolen breeches.

Sophia prayed the heat she felt in her face was not translating into bright red cheeks.

"I do not know," the gentleman said. "I would certainly riot to see them again."

"Ah, I see you two do not know each other," said Harry, performing what Sophia considered a pretty poor rescue. "Philip Egerton, Earl of Marnmouth, 'tis my pleasure to introduce you to Miss Sophia Worsley, a friend of mine."

Sophia swallowed. *The Earl of Marnmouth.* Well, she had heard the rumors, of course. Everyone had. And an earl. Despite her friendship with Harry, these were not circles in which she typically moved. They were friends, to be sure, but they were both intelligent enough to understand that there were places Harry was welcome that Sophia simply was not.

"Sophia Worsley," said the earl, and Sophia shivered to hear her name on his lips. "Now, I know that name."

And just as things were starting to get a little interesting, it would all come tumbling down, thought Sophia. If she could go through the rest of her life never being recognized as the lady in society who has been jilted at the altar not once but twice, she would be delighted.

But that did not look likely to happen. It was most unfair, but then, she had expected it.

She shifted slightly on her feet, ready for the teasing onslaught, and she felt the tightness of the breeches on her legs. It was time to change the conversation.

"You probably do know that name," she said as airily as she could manage. "But I have never heard of you."

Sophia almost saw the sparks flying from the earl's eyes as he beheld her with a smile.

"Really?" he said softly. "I will have to amend that immediately."

"I do not see why," said Sophia, ignoring the frantic motions of Harry behind the earl's back. "I have no interest in you.

Her words shocked even her. She had never been this bold before, never spoken to a gentleman like this. But he *made* her bold. The

Earl of Marnmouth was grinning, and it was astonishing how much more attractive that smile made him.

"But I am greatly interested in you, Miss Sophia Worsley," he said in a low, sultry voice. "More interested than anyone else here, which is saying something. Why, the whole place cannot stop looking at you."

With great restraint, Sophia broke the connection of their gazes and looked around. He was right. Although there were ladies averting their eyes and whispering hurriedly to their friends, there were a more significant number of gentlemen eyeing her, as though she was the next course to be served at a feast.

"Perhaps," she said as calmly as she could manage. "But their interest in me does not automatically translate into my own interest. Gentlemen may look at me all they wish."

"Sophia," Harry began. "I think—"

She was not permitted to continue. In a swift movement that made Sophia gasp, the earl grabbed her hand and pulled her away from her party.

Thanking her stars she was wearing gloves, for Sophia did not want the heat of his fingers directly on her skin, she tried to catch her breath as the reckless man pulled her past gaggles of people until they stopped in a recess hidden by a large plant.

"All right, damn you, you have my attention," said the earl. He was hardly out of breath, while Sophia could barely catch her own. "Though I do not know why you did it this way. I can offer you a good income if you prove as delectable as you look."

His words simply did not make sense. *Delectable? Good income? What on earth was the confused earl talking about?*

Sophia was not a woman of the world, but she had spent more than a few Seasons in society, and her heart started to flutter most painfully as she realized what he meant.

He—he was propositioning her! He meant to make her his mistress! If she had not been so offended, Sophia would have been flattered.

Pulling her fingers from his, she said coldly, "You have greatly misunderstood, sir."

"Have I? Have I, indeed," said the earl. His voice was low and deep, and Sophia found herself taking a step closer. "You did not wish to gain the attention of the most handsome and most powerful men in the room? For you have."

Sophia took a small step toward him. It was impossible not to. Here was a man, not like Jacob, who was more a boy. She could not understand it, and she could not stay here long. Not if she wanted her heart to remain in her chest.

"I am not to be bought," she breathed, not

taking her eyes from his. "Nor taken in."

If anything, the earl looked even more pleased. "Not interested in being a mistress, then. What about a wife?"

For a moment, Sophia was sure she had misheard him. *No, this could not be happening—not again.* She had walked down this path before, and she knew what lay at the end. *Nothing but misery.*

"I have been jilted before, sir, and have no interest in matrimony," she said formally. "Now go away."

Turning on her heels and forcing herself not to look back at the striking man, Sophia was surprised to find Harry waiting on the other side of the large fronds of the plant.

"Harry, why did you leave me to be—be *accosted* by your friend!" Sophia could not help but sound a little accusing.

But Harry did not look abashed. On the contrary, she was laughing. "Why not? You appeared to be having so much fun."

CHAPTER FOUR

*H*OW ON EARTH *had he managed to get dragged into this?* Here he was, an earl of the realm, more education and knowledge of the world than half the people in the room put together—and he was stuck in a corner with Miss Olivia Lymington?

"—and what a fine fabric it is," she was saying, her eyes glazed over as she described her twin sister's wedding gown. "So delicate, so fine—it took Isabella more than three months to find precisely the fabric she was looking…"

Marnmouth stifled a yawn and wondered whether he could tilt his head to see the clock over the mantelpiece in Mrs. Marnion's drawing room—but no.

He did not need to see a clock, however. He knew he had been here almost an hour and was damned if he was going to stand here much longer.

"Miss Lymington," he began, but he was utterly flattened by her monologue.

"Few people are able to distinguish between…"

Usually, he would not have minded. After all, Miss Lymington, like her identical twin sister, was a rather splendid thing to look at. Chestnut hair with just a twist of a smile always dancing on those kissable lips—if he was someone younger, more foolish… *Braedon came to mind*, Marnmouth thought with a smile, *he would be utterly taken in. As it was…*

"The hem!" said Miss Lymington. "I have not seen anything to match it. Of course, the veil itself is more a piece of magic and mystery than fine English needlework. When my mother found…"

Marnmouth nodded absentmindedly and darted a quick look around the room, seeing with a sinking heart that it barely mattered whether or not he was able to extricate himself from Miss Lymington—not when he had no other prospects before him.

Why had he assented to attend Mrs. Marnion's card party? Because he had received no better offers. It was another depressing thought, but not one he could escape.

He was getting old. He was starting to feel old. There was an uncomfortable twinge in his lower back if he tried to get out of bed at speed which had never been there before.

In his youth, he would be inundated with requests for his presence across town—and out of town. Shooting parties, hunts, card games, rides, duels…

Now all he had this entire week was this damned card party.

It appeared he was one of the few gentlemen who had returned their invitation card with the affirmative. The small card tables Mrs. Marnion's butler had ably spaced around the room were packed with the best names, all married ladies or ladies desperate for his attention.

"—such shoes as befitting a future duchess," Miss Lymington continued, utterly oblivious that she had lost her companion's attention a long time ago. "I have only…"

"Yes, yes," muttered Marnmouth. He had no wish for Miss Lymington to know that she bored him senseless—he was no cad.

If only he could enjoy some hearty conversation about something…*actually important*. One of the few gentlemen who had answered Mrs. Marnion's call appeared to be Axwick, but he was keeping close to his wife.

Marnmouth was no expert, far from it, but based on his friend's attention, there would soon be an announcement of another small Axwick joining the family in the next few months.

Then there was a gentleman he knew by

name but knew his wife better, hence his invitation to their wedding just a week before. Jacob Beauvale. There was some sort of scandal, he knew but had never inquired further.

Until today. When he heard the scandal involved Miss Sophia Worsley, he had—delicately, of course—charged his butler to ascertain all the relevant details.

Miss Sophia Worsley. He had forced that intoxicating wench from his mind the moment she had stepped away from him at Almack's, but she had the infuriating ability to force herself back into his thoughts at any given opportunity.

The gossip had been scant on the ground, but two facts remained. Firstly, Miss Worsley had been engaged for a period of more than a twelvemonth to Jacob. Secondly, the man had married Mrs. Howard.

It was easy to see why. There was Mrs. Howard now, dazzling blonde hair and a pretty smile even Marnmouth was not immune to. And the Howard name was prestigious; everyone knew that.

But a year's engagement...a commitment usually as secure as one's wedding vows. A broken engagement of that length was genuinely scandalous. No wonder Miss Worsley was...

"I am not to be bought. Nor taken in."

"You know, I think 'tis Isabella's devotion to ensuring every detail is precisely correct. That is why their engagement has lingered on so," Miss Lymington's voice cut through his thoughts on engagements with one of her own.

Marnmouth nodded. "Hmm. Yes."

Only then did he realize where he had heard the name Lymington before. Poor old Larnwick—the duke who had attended his dinner a few weeks ago. Miss Isabella Lymington, the twin of the Lymington standing before him, would be marrying him.

Poor man, he thought fervently. *If the elder Miss Lymington is anything like the twin he was conversing with, it would be a very dull marriage. But then, would that be any different from other marriages?*

Marnmouth's dark eyes swept around the room packed with ladies who had decided, diplomatically, of course, to leave their husbands at home. *Why? Were they bored of them already?*

Jacob Beauvale—now he did interest him. *What sort of a gentleman could spend a year in the proximity of the delectable Miss Worsley—those eyes, the way her breeches had tightened around her buttocks—and decide not to marry her?*

"You must excuse me, Miss Lymington," he said and saw the hurt on the young lady's face. "Though I could stand here and talk with you for hours to my heart's content, I am afraid duty and honor require me to speak with Beauvale. You will, naturally, forgive me."

Bowing low and kissing the hand immediately proffered to him, Marnmouth smiled charmingly, released the hand, and stepped away.

Still, there was disappointment on Miss Lymington's face. *She probably*, Marnmouth thought with a wry smile, *hoped to nab him for a husband.*

His title was not as impressive as the duke her twin sister was marrying. But then the engagement had been dragging on something terrible if the gossips were to be believed. Perhaps Miss Olivia Lymington hoped to step down the aisle before Miss Isabella. It would not be the first sibling outrage to grace the gossip columns.

It took only a little weaving in and out of ladies for Marnmouth to reach the other side of the room and bow to the couple who had seated themselves to watch the card players.

"Beauvale," Marnmouth inclined his head, "the Honorable Mrs. Beauvale."

As he straightened up, he examined Mrs. Beauvale, who had been the Honorable Mrs. Elmore Howard. He had met that brigand of her first husband only once and had sought never to do so again. *What a cad. What an absolute idiot.*

On the other hand, his wife, now Beauvale's wife, looked far more intelligent and benevolent. Swollen with child and with a very pretty face, she smiled.

"You will forgive me if I do not rise, your lordship," she said. "It was an honor to have you at our wedding. Let me introduce you formally to my husband. Philip Egerton, Earl of Marnmouth, Jacob Beauvale."

Marnmouth bowed again, and Beauvale rose from his seat hastily and bowed himself.

"I must congratulate you," said Marnmouth. "Your first child, and so soon after your marriage. Congratulations to you both."

Was it his imagination, or did Beauvale look puzzled? His wife nudged his leg as he was still standing.

"Oh—oh, yes, first child," Beauvale said hastily, pushing his hair out of his eyes with a grin. "Yes. Thank you."

Marnmouth forced himself not to smile. *The man was exactly how he had imagined. Well-meaning, but not the brightest button in the box.*

Even he, in London, when it had occurred in Bath, heard the rumors of Mrs. Howard, now Mrs. Beauvale's, first child. It was all very suspicious, and the more she claimed her son was the child of her first husband, the less society believed her.

Well, who was he to judge? He had at least three children on the wrong side of the blanket. He looked after them and their mothers, of course, but still. *These things happened.*

"Yes, Lizzy—my wife has been marvelous during her pregnancy," Beauvale wittered on, eyes bright as he looked at his wife. "I would never choose to undergo it myself, not after seeing the discomfort of it all, yet she continues without a complaint…"

Marnmouth found, to his horror, he had merely swapped one monologue of absolutely no interest to him for another.

He was sick to death of it all. Pretension from the ladies, lies from the gentlemen—it was a wonder anyone got anything done at all. Everyone lies, simpers, pretends. If he was not careful, he would find himself trapped here for the rest of the night. *Time to make an escape.*

"—names are always difficult, but we thought if 'tis a girl—"

"You must excuse me, Beauvale," interrupted Marnmouth as delicately as he could. "It is pleasant to make your acquaintance, and to see you again, Mrs. How—my apologies, Mrs. Beauvale. I must retrieve something from my greatcoat."

Without waiting for a response, he bowed and strode away into the relative calm of the hallway.

It was cooler here, almost silent. Marnmouth took a deep breath and let it out slowly.

Christ alive, but one could not pay him enough to go back in there. He was fortunate to only be there a few hours. Some poor souls wouldn't escape Mrs. Marnion's clutches until the early hours.

"Your greatcoat, my lord?"

Marnmouth turned around and smiled as a footman stepped forward with his coat.

"Very insightful, I must say," said Marnmouth with a smile. "Thank you."

Taking the greatcoat from the servant's hands, he started toward the door.

"May I take a message to my lady?"

Marnmouth hesitated. *Yes, it would be awfully bad form to simply stride out of the house without leaving a placating message for the lady of the house.*

"Yes," he said curtly. "Fashion it as you would—great apologies, forced to leave against my will, duty calls, that sort of thing."

He could not ignore the look of stern disapproval on the footman's face as he closed the door behind him, but what did it matter? *He was the Earl of Marnmouth.* He did not have to send apologies to a mere Mrs. who felt slighted as he left after ten o'clock in the evening.

The night air was fresh. He had been buried alive in Mrs. Marnion's card party, forced to listen to the inane nonsense of ladies all around him.

The night, however, was still relatively young even if he was not, and there was a burning itch within him to do something with it. He did not wish to simply trip home and fold himself into his bed linens like an old man.

Besides, Mrs. Marnion's home was only a few streets over from...

It was ten minutes of brisk walking, but

Marnmouth did not mind. By the time he had arrived, he was warmed through and perfectly ready to give the password. The door he was looking for was an ordinary door in a typical street.

Marnmouth smiled. *He knew better than that.*

The smart rapping on the door caused a slat to move. Bright candlelight poured from it, and then a face appeared in the gap, blocking out most of the light.

"And?"

Marnmouth cleared his throat. "God save the Queen."

The slat shot back, leaving him in darkness, but not for long. The door opened, and Marnmouth was beckoned to enter the Queen of Hearts.

Stepping down the corridor, he walked the well-worn path—curving to the left, and then the right, until it opened up into the large gambling den.

"God save you, y'lordship," said the proprietor, a weaselly looking man with few teeth spreading into a wide grin. "The Queen of Hearts is not a place for a gentleman."

Marnmouth smiled. "Which is why I find myself here so often."

Everything about the Queen of Hearts made him relax. In many ways, it was the complete opposite of Mrs. Marnion's restrained and quiet card party. Here there were no ladies but plenty of wine, cigar smoke billowing around the room, and raucous arguments occurring at some tables as disagreements were settled by the fist or, if it came to it, the blade.

Here, at least, was a place he could tell someone they were boring without them bursting into tears.

There were a few empty seats at most tables, and he stepped around the room to see the different games being played—almost falling back in shock as he beheld one of the players.

Miss Sophia Worsley. Miss Sophia Worsley once again wearing those breeches which tightened and defined every inch of her body. How did she learn of this place? Of course, a rebel would know, and that was exactly what this delightful woman wanted to be. He would not ask her, some secrets were better kept.

He stopped, just out of her sightline, and took her in. *By God, but he would have her if he could, mistress or no.* Looking at her made parts of him—a rather significant part—swell and stand to attention. *If the rest of her was anything like her buttocks…*

Marnmouth swallowed. He had come to the Queen of Hearts to escape the ladies, and yet here she was, the one lady dancing in his thoughts since he had last seen her.

Who could blame him for such a reaction? He was no monk and had no mistress for years now.

Emma Tilbury was pretty enough, in her own way, but Sophia was a woman he could sink into and never wish to leave. *By God, she was so sweet. She was—*

"Goodness, hello, Marnmouth," said Miss Worsley.

Marnmouth blinked and realized he had been standing there like a fool as the people at the table stared at him, including Miss Worsley. *Damn.*

"Did you wish to be cut into this hand?" she asked with a smile. "We have just dealt."

Marnmouth found himself uncontrollably pulled toward her. He simply could not resist. *Who could? What in God's name was she doing here?*

Nodding without saying a word, he sat in the empty seat beside Miss Worsley and had three cards thrust at him by a man with a scarred cheek.

"Half a crown."

Marnmouth blinked at the man.

Miss Worsley laughed raucously. "Come now, Marnmouth, you have surely played before! The blind, sir, is half a crown. If you do not have it, I can lend it to you."

Cursing under his breath at how easily this damned woman could intoxicate him, he threw the coin down, and the game began.

As the betting started on the other side of the table, he took his chance to murmur under his breath, "I had not expected to find you in a place like this."

She did not appear offended. "Rather here than Mrs. Marnion's card party, I can assure you. I assume that is where you have come from?"

Marnmouth nodded. *How was it possible a young lady of relatively good family could find herself here, in the Queen of Hearts, and look more at ease than he did?*

He glanced at his cards. *Nothing. Time to bluff then.*

The betting reached Sophia and had grown another half-crown. Marnmouth watched her bite her lip ever so slightly in the corner, and his stomach lurched on her behalf.

She was nervous, and rightly so! This was a gambling den, not a card party with the best of society. There were thieves, cutthroats, and petty criminals here.

She needed to be careful.

It was fortunate he was here to protect her. Marnmouth swallowed. He had the feeling she would not wish for it, anyway. No, at this point, he was simply a card player at the same table as Miss Sophia Worsley.

A Miss Sophia Worsley in breeches.

Marnmouth tried his absolute best not to glance down, take another look at her, and instead folded. "Too rich for my blood," he said aloud.

Miss Worsley laughed. "So says the earl!

Well, if that is what you wish. Show your hands then, gentlemen."

From where did this confidence come? Marnmouth knew he should pay attention to the hands being revealed by the brigands at the table—he could then calculate who had been bluffing to predict it in the next.

But all he wanted to look at was Sophia. *By God, she was intoxicating.*

"Two pair, nines and fours," smirked the scarred man. "Read them and weep, boys."

The other man at the table sighed heavily. "And I thought three fives would have taken it. Go on, then, take your winnings."

The scarred man reached out and started to pull the pile of coins in the middle of the table toward him.

"Ah, excuse me."

The entire table turned to look at Miss Worsley, who was smiling. "I think you are taking my winnings, sir."

With a flourish, she laid down her cards—a royal flush. She grinned at Marnmouth, who could not help but return the smile.

Christ alive. What was she doing here? She was robbing them, somehow, of all their coin! 'Twas a risky idea, of course, but when one could place down a royal flush…

What had that fool Beauvale been thinking, letting her go? He would probably marry her on the spot if she offered herself to him.

"Royal flush be damned, that's a cheaters hand," growled the scarred man.

Miss Worsley bristled. "How dare you accuse me of—"

"Now, gentlemen, I think it is clear the lady won fair and square," said Marnmouth hastily. He did not want to see a fistfight, not with Miss Worsley here.

She was concentrating, however, on getting every single coin into her reticule. "And that is all for now, gentlemen, so you gain a reprieve. I am sure I will see you again soon."

Rising, she tried to step away from the table but couldn't. Marnmouth, instinctively and without thought, had taken her arm. "Let me walk you home."

The words had escaped his mouth before he was conscious they had done so. Miss Worsley, walking home, alone, in London? *He could not countenance it.*

She, however, glared at his hand on her arm. He dropped it quickly.

"Really, sir," she said with a sardonic smile. "I have lived in London almost all of my life. I know it well enough."

Marnmouth glanced at the two men she had beaten soundly at the table, and resolved to go with her. *If they decided to follow her…*

"Still, I would prefer it," he said firmly.

"Goodbye, gentlemen, well played."

He took hold of her arm once more and did not let go until they had stepped out of the secret door and into the freezing night air.

"Goodness, you are feeling heroic today, are you not?"

Marnmouth had not been expecting such a retort. Gratitude, perhaps. Maybe even a little flattery. *But this?* Miss Worsley was looking at him almost pitying, as though he had been forced to do something foolish.

"I have no need of you," said Miss Worsley, tucking her reticule under her arm. "'Tis not far for me to return home, and—"

"I am perfectly aware you have no need of me," Marnmouth interrupted. "Needing me is not interesting. I have no wish to be merely needed. I want to be needed *and* wanted."

His breath had blossomed out in the night air, and Sophia—*he must consider her Miss Worsley, this was most irregular*—was looking at him warily.

"I only live a few streets away," she said.

Marnmouth nodded. "Good. Time for you to tell me about a gentleman I met today."

Miss Worsley had already started walking, but he had caught up with her as she laughed. "A gentleman? How wild do you think I am, that I know every gentleman in London?"

"I am sure you know this one," countered Marnmouth. "A Mr. Beauvale?"

Sophia stopped dead and glared. "What have you been—why are you inquiring into my past, my lord? What business it is of yours who I have been…you are *infuriating*."

Her last words were almost spat as Marnmouth grinned. *Why, if this was the reaction whenever he riled up Sophia Worsley, he would be doing it far more often.*

"I am infuriating," he admitted cheerfully as they crossed a silent street. "And yet you are far more infuriating and intoxicating than I am. My God, Sophia, those breeches. Where in Heaven's name did you find them?"

He was somewhat restrained for not touching her bottom, which begged to be cupped by his hands—but he was prevented by Sophia, who pushed him off the pavement.

"I should have known that was all you were intrigued by," she said coldly. "Well, we are only a street away from my home, and so I shall tell you that Beauvale and I were engaged, and now we are not. You can go away now."

Like hell. Marnmouth was not sure how he would ever leave her. His mind was perplexed, utterly overwhelmed. His senses were consumed, and all he could think of was Miss Sophia Worsley.

"Thank you for that information," he said aloud. "And I am glad we are only one street away. Every step takes us closer to the moment when I will kiss you."

There it was. Finally, he was able to make her blush. Even in the darkness of the night, he could not mistake those pink cheeks for anything else. She was a marvel. The opposite of dull, the tonic to the boredom of the world.

Sophia Worsley. What a woman.

"I will not allow you to kiss me," she said fiercely, attempting to increase her pace.

Marnmouth matched it. "You will want me to, Sophia. Trust me."

She laughed into the silent night. "My word, you are very sure of yourself. What makes you think that?"

He had not planned it. It was simply an out-working of the passion growing in his soul, and though he knew he would not have her that night, it was time to treat Miss Sophia Worsley to a little taste of what he could offer.

Without saying a word, he suddenly stepped back onto the pavement and pushed her against the wall.

"What—"

"Because," he breathed into her ear, his chest pressed up against hers as he fought the urge to groan at the sensation of her breasts, "because you will want to know. You will wonder what it is like to kiss me, and when you get home, you will lie awake aching for the knowledge."

Marnmouth could feel her shiver against him

and knew she wanted him—or at least, something from him. Her body betrayed her, and he lifted his head to look into her eyes. They were bright, fierce, and did not look away.

"You speak a lot of a nonsense for an earl," she breathed.

He grinned. "Unless you ask me, Sophia, you will never know what it is to kiss me, and will have to live always wondering."

It took every ounce of his self-control not to crush his lips onto hers. *How was he ever to resist her as she struggled and pressed even harder against him?*

Her eyes met his. "Kiss me."

He needed no further invitation. Hands around her waist, Marnmouth's lips captured her own and poured down all the passion, the frustration, the desire, and wonder that she sparked in him. *And by God, she returned it.* Her hands were around his neck, clinging to him as she utterly allowed him in.

Eventually, he had no choice but to break the kiss. "Christ, Sophia, I want to bed you."

"It meant nothing," she said quietly. "Do not expect anything else, Marnmouth. You said I wanted to know—well, now I know."

Marnmouth struggled to think, his mind so awash with the heady memories of that kiss. *Nothing else? How could she say that?*

"I have sworn off men, off matrimony," she

said lightly, pushing him away.

He staggered backward. It was a surprise his legs could still hold him.

"Goodnight," Sophia said lightly as she walked down the street, hips moving in a sultry pattern made even worse by the tightness of her breeches.

Marnmouth leaned against the wall. *Christ alive. Her words only made him more eager.* "You little rebel," he breathed with a smile. "We'll see how long your resolve lasts."

CHAPTER FIVE

SOPHIA ATTEMPTED TO quash her irritation as she said, "But I do not wish to!"

It appeared that she had been unsuccessful. Her mother's face appeared around the edge of her bedchamber door, and it did not look happy.

"And I have said before, this is not a debate," she said with far more strength of feeling. "The Lymingtons will be here in half an hour, and you will join me to entertain them."

Sophia rolled her eyes. *Another set of idiotic ladies visiting her mother, and she was forced to entertain them!*

"I cannot think of anything worse," she said in a defiant tone. *How was she to escape the monotony of society?* One would think, after passing her majority and then surpassing it, she would be permitted to do what she wished with her time.

"I certainly can," her mother said tartly, "and

I will ensure you do, too, if you are not careful. Now heed me well, Sophia, for I will not say this again. Get dressed, earbobs in, ribbon in your hair, and then downstairs. As quick as you can!"

"But I have no wish to—"

"I will see you in ten minutes!"

The door snapped shut, and the only sound in the house was the slightly irate noise of her mother stomping down the stairs—a habit she had gifted to her only child.

Sophia sighed heavily as she leaned back in her chair by her toilette. Her looking glass shone back, showing a lady with tired eyes in her nightgown.

Sophia had no wish to sit through another hour of nonsense from her parents.

"Oh, if you only curled your hair this way…"

"Perhaps if you had worn more white gowns, Jacob would have…"

"I think we should try this particular cream, look at how…"

Sophia picked up her hairbrush and started to attack her curls fiercely. It was all her parents cared about, her marriage, and it did not seem to matter that she had utterly given up any chance that would occur.

Now the Lymingtons were coming, some of the most irritating and dull people she ever had the misfortune to meet.

How was she supposed to entertain the friends of

her parents and their daughters with the memory of Marnmouth's kiss still dancing on her lips?

Sophia closed her eyes and was transported back to that moment, just two nights ago. She could feel the roughness of the bricks against her back, the chill of the wind, and the heat in her chest as she was trapped—but not by his body, by his presence.

"Kiss me."

A smile crept over her face. She had been wrong to ask for that kiss.

"Because you will want to know. You will wonder what it is like to kiss me, and when you get home, you will lie awake aching for the knowledge."

And he had been right. The Earl of Marnmouth, despite being a good ten or so years older than herself, had not lost any of his charm.

To the contrary. He was so unlike these...these boys who were at so many of the dances she attended. Foolish, stammering, childish things.

The earl was all man in a heady way that did strange things to her.

She had wanted him, desired him in a way she had never wanted a gentleman before. Even the foolish kisses she had bestowed upon Jacob during their courtship and engagement—none of them had made her want to cling to him.

But Philip—Marnmouth, that was...

He did something to her she could not understand. Rebellious, but not in the way she had intended.

"I have sworn off men, off matrimony."

Sophia opened her eyes. There was no getting around it; she had been foolish. Now the poor man would think all he had to do was taunt her a little, and she would willingly allow him to…well. *Do whatever he wanted.*

But she was resolute. She was tired of all this nonsense around matrimony. It was as she had told Lady Romeril, over a year ago now, when the elderly woman had demanded she marry.

"I do not see why I should. Why should I? My life is most agreeable as it is, and I see no reason to change it. I have all the money and connections I need. That is why most ladies marry, is it not? But I am quite content as I am."

Sophia glanced at the gown her mother's lady's maid had laid out, so typical of her mother's style. Demure, the bodice designed to be loose, sleeves right down to her wrists.

Ten minutes later, she stepped into the drawing room to a gasp from her mother.

Mr. Worsley turned around. "Not this again!"

Sophia smiled innocently and took a seat by the fireplace. "I cannot imagine what you mean, Father."

"Well, really!" breathed her mother, glancing at her husband.

"Mother was very clear in her instructions," said Sophia, crossing one leg over the other in the breeches she had now permanently borrowed from their long-suffering butler. "Mother said to get dressed, put on earbobs, weave a ribbon into my hair—and I have obeyed."

Rolling his eyes, he said, "You are being deliberately difficult!"

Sophia shrugged. "Yes, probably, but what difference does it make? The Lymingtons have already seen me like this. They won't care."

"They have already seen—"

"Yes, well," Mrs. Worsley interrupted her husband hastily, telling Sophia her mother had not thought to inform him about that particular escapade. "The point is, Sophia, that they will see you again! Almack's was just a blip, I am sure, and—"

"Almack's!"

Mrs. Worsley winced. She had evidently not intended to let that particular word slip.

"I thought you turning up at Jacob's wedding in those damned things was bad enough," said Mr. Worsley, his face starting to go red, "but Almack's!"

Sophia swallowed. "Well, I was not wearing this pair of breeches at the Beauvale wedding. I actually borrowed—"

"You think I care which pair of breeches it was?" Her father was breathing heavily now. "I never thought I would have such a rebellious daughter. No wonder you are unmarried!"

His words were unusually stern. *Why did her parents have to conflate every single mistake she made to the fact that her engagements had not led to matrimony?*

"'Tis not my fault my engagement to Jacob was broken off," she said stiffly. "Nor the first."

Mr. Worsley laughed dryly. "Well, dressed like that, 'tis no wonder Robert and Jacob did not wish to marry you!"

After his words, there was a ringing silence in the room. Mrs. Worsley looked shocked, but Sophia did not look away from her father's gaze.

She had known it, of course. She had known her parents too long to believe their kind words when Jacob had stormed away, right at the altar in the church.

They blamed her, at least in part. But she had not done anything rebellious until *after* Jacob had abandoned her. How could they blame her for not wanting to marry after being so brutally jilted?

"You always promised," she said quietly, "you promised you would never blame me for that—that neither of them were my fault."

Her mother glanced at Mr. Worsley and looked as though she was going to say something, but before she could, he spoke again.

"I know," he said heavily. "But I never thought you would be this…this!" He gestured at her, averting his eyes from her legs. "Where in

God's name did you get them from, anyway?"

Sophia could not help it. "I may have borrowed them from our delightful butler."

Mrs. Worsley sighed. "Sophia Worsley, you have not! The poor man thought he was coming near to the end of his time, mislaying his clothes left, right, and center! Really!"

A knock at the door ceased their discussion immediately.

"Lord, the Lymingtons are here," Mrs. Worsley said distractedly, glancing at the clock on the mantelpiece. "And they are early!"

Mr. Worsley did not look so flustered. He was looking at his daughter sternly, and Sophia could not help but feel a little abashed. "Upstairs, gown, now."

Sophia rose and stomped upstairs. Over twenty-one years of age and could not wear what she wanted. It was always her parents' friends and their daughters she had to entertain. No wonder she was bored to tears.

When was she to have her own life, her own choices?

Holding back from the temptation to slam her bedchamber door, she fell onto her bed in silent fury.

She knew the answer, of course. *She would never have any sort of mastery over her own life, until—or unless—she married.* She would always be her parents' daughter or a man's wife. Never her own person, never making her own decisions. It was enough to make one want to run away and marry an Irish lord, like Miss Mariah Wynn.

Sophia did not know her well, but they had been in the same circles. Miss Wynn had rarely been seen, of course, except behind a book. A bluestocking through and through, no one had thought she would ever marry—but Viscount Donal had seen something in her.

Perhaps she should go to Ireland to find a husband who didn't care about such things.

Even then, she would still be someone's wife and not her own person.

Well, she could not simply lie here forever. Murmured chatter drifted up the stairs. The Lymingtons had been welcomed into the drawing room directly below her bedchamber.

Pulling off the offending breeches and forcing herself into a gown with great difficulty, choosing not to call a maid in, Sophia tried not to stomp too loudly downstairs as she entered the drawing room to entertain the Miss Lymingtons and their mother.

She had to force a smile as they all turned to look at her and then continued on with their conversations. *If only she could escape this nightmare.* If only she had pretended to have a prior engagement with Harry! That would have been the clever thing to do, but instead, she was stuck here.

Her mother was seated on the other side of the room beside Mrs. Lymington, the two mothers clucking away about their daughters.

The Miss Lymington Sophia recognized, Olivia, was standing by the fireplace. She was talking animatedly to her father, who already had that glazed look about him.

The elder Miss Lymington, for although they were twins, there were small differences if one knew where to look, was seated alone on a sofa with a cup of tea.

Sophia sat beside Isabella and smiled. "Miss Lymington," she said politely if a little stiffly. "How pleasant to finally make your acquaintance."

She inclined her head gracefully. She was very pretty, Sophia had to admit, but there was something...*cold* in her manner.

"Yes, I suppose it is," said Miss Lymington. Her sister glanced at her with pink cheeks but said nothing as her twin continued, "and I have heard much about you, Miss Worsley. A great deal."

Sophia smiled mechanically. *So, it was to be like that, was it?* "Your wedding plans with the Duke of Larnwick continue, I hear?"

It was a safe subject. Surely Miss Lymington would wish to talk about it—everyone was.

"I would have thought you would not wish to talk about matrimony after your two debacles."

Sophia swallowed. She was entertaining guests, and more importantly, her parents' guests. She needed to stay calm.

"I do not mind," she said, keeping a smile plastered on her face. "I can talk about it easily enough."

"My word, I admire your fortitude," said Miss Lymington with just a hint of sarcasm. "That is indeed impressive. I mean to say, two gentlemen have decided they have no wish to marry you after engagements. What about you decided them against you, do you think?"

The absolute cheek of the girl! How dare she speak like that to her, and in her own home, too!

But it was clear Miss Lymington, unlike her younger twin, believed she could say whatever she wanted, and Sophia was not going to dishonor and disgrace her parents.

"Each situation was so different," she said quietly. "I hardly know where to begin. It is more pleasant to talk of other things. Have you visited the Larnwick estate in Scotland?"

But it appeared the nosey Miss Lymington had no interest in her own life. "Tell me all about it, Miss Worsley, I must know. Did they not like you wearing breeches? I was fair shocked, seeing you at Almack's. Did they rescind your vouchers, tear them up?"

Sophia took a deep breath and remembered

why she had not wanted to entertain the Lymingtons in the first place. *Miss Olivia was perhaps a little foolish, a little too easily swayed by prestige—but her sister?*

Miss Olivia was to be preferred over this one. The elder twin was mean, selfish, and did not seem to have any comprehension of what an appropriate question was!

Sophia would not let her get the better of her. "I may be a little rebellious, but—"

"A bit!" Miss Lymington's words were so loud that her father glanced over from the fireplace. "Quite a lot, I would say. I am not surprised no gentleman wants to marry you."

Sophia had a retort ready, but while it would have been acceptable at the Queen of Hearts, it was not one she could voice here.

Besides, she had been rebellious enough this week. The image of Philip—the Earl of Marnmouth—appeared in her mind, and she smiled, all the tension from her irritating conversation with Miss Lymington fading anyway.

She had to put him out of her mind.

"I always think," she said airily, "some gentlemen like a little rebelliousness."

Was that a pout of irritation from Miss Lymington? "Not my intended. The Duke of Larnwick is a very handsome, wealthy man, and…"

And that was when she utterly lost Sophia's attention. Finally able to find a topic that did not disparage her hosts' daughter, Miss Lymington started talking away, and Sophia nodded a few times to keep her on the same foolish topic.

Anything to avoid more personal criticisms of all her life choices. Besides, she had plenty to think about.

Philip. The Earl of Marnmouth, she corrected silently. Here was a gentleman who desired her, and desired her for...her. She had a pleasing dowry, that was true, but Robert had needed far more, and Jacob had only been attempting to fulfill the requirements of that strange codicil.

But Philip...he saw her and wanted her.

She must not allow herself to be alone with him again, or she may ask him to kiss her again— and where would that lead?

CHAPTER SIX

THE DART THAT flew from Marnmouth's hand soared across the room and stuck firmly into the wall.

He did not even look around to see what he had hit. The dartboard had been taken down weeks ago after it had almost collapsed, pricked with holes from his years of accuracy. Now he just threw his darts at the wall. *What did it matter?* He had plenty of money to have the wall replastered.

Bored, bored, bored.

Three days. Three days since he'd seen Sophia, since he'd pinned her against that wall and drew out of her that honest request.

And that kiss…

Marnmouth fell onto the sofa in his study. A vision crowded his mind of Sophia, the woman panting under his touch, desperate—despite her fine words—for another kiss.

He had been certain she would have sought him out by now. Yes, she had protested about not wishing for matrimony, but he had felt her quiver under his touch. She had reached out for him, asked for the kiss he had bestowed so willingly.

And yet, she had not appeared. *It was maddening!*

So here he was, stuck at home. It was not exactly a hardship. The Marnmouth London house was finer than most in the city.

He had friends, acquaintances, even enemies who would all welcome him to their table.

Wasn't it foolish of him, a man she probably laughed at, to think that she would call?

Idiot man. The night had fallen hours ago, and candles flickered in his study.

Well, thought a sarcastic part of his mind he ignored at every opportunity, *there was always Emma.*

He pushed the thought away. *Yes, it was tempting to fall back into the tender arms of Emma Tilbury.* When one knew the pleasure she could give, it was indeed enticing.

But he could not go back. He had stuck to his principles in the two years since he had broken with her, and he would not rescind his word.

"If you just give me a few minutes, I am sure I can convince you."

Marnmouth sat up and sighed heavily. No, he would not permit himself to fall back into old habits, even now he was past his fortieth year. Life was nothing if one did not move forward to new things, and he was determined to do just that.

New things like Sophia.

Sophia had wanted him. She had taken his kiss, then left him.

For all his fine words about needing and wanting, Sophia sparked a strange mixture of both in him whenever he was in her presence.

He almost laughed. *The two times he had been in her presence!* This was wild, this was madness. *When had a miss ever done this to him?*

He felt useless. Most ladies her age were desperate for husbands. He had heard the rumors. He knew from her own lips that she had been jilted. *But how many ladies endured that and turned up to Almack's in breeches?*

She was one in a million. Perhaps rarer. Miss Sophia Worsley was going to crowd his mind and haunt his dreams if he did not get what he wanted.

The study door opened, and McCall appeared, looking rather stiff. A flicker of guilt moved through Marnmouth. He really should look into getting some sort of pension sorted out for his old butler. *The man had served almost forty years. The poor thing needed a break.*

"Most of the servants have returned from their days off, my lord," said the butler formally.

"I was going to lock up the property now. Are you about to retire?"

Marnmouth glanced at the clock. It was just past ten o'clock in the evening, and yet already he could feel the tug of tiredness around his eyes.

By God, there was a time when he would consider ten o'clock in the evening the time to start an adventure!

A spontaneous choice rushed through his mind. "No, McCall, I am going out. Lock the door behind me. I will take a key."

Gambling would take his mind off her, he decided as he pocketed a front door key and strode out into the chilling night. A few hands of cards would do him nicely, allow him to settle, and then when he came home, he could go to bed.

"God save the Queen," he muttered to the faceless doorkeeper behind the slat, and within a minute, he was down in the belly of the place—where a terrible scene unfolded.

A table had been overturned in the middle of the room, with cards and coins scattered all over the place. Two men were jeering at a third man holding someone in his arms.

Marnmouth's heart went cold. *Sophia.* She was struggling against the man, but she was not strong enough to cast him off entirely. The other gentlemen in the Queen of Hearts were laughing, viewing her as their entertainment for the evening.

He reacted before he was able to think. Roaring like a lion, Marnmouth ran forward and pulled the man from Sophia, pushing him to the floor.

"I will kill you," Marnmouth panted heavily, his eyes narrowed as he glared at the miscreant, "if you ever touch her again. Do you hear me? I said, do you hear me?"

The man nodded hastily, backing away.

Marnmouth was only then aware that Sophia had clung onto him, tucked into his arms. *If he had not decided to come here tonight...*

The thought was not to be borne. It was intolerable. *Would he have to set up an armed guard around this woman?*

As though able to hear his thoughts, Sophia pulled away. He could see genuine fear in her eyes, but there was no quiver in her voice as she spoke. "I do not need your help."

"Like hell you don't," Marnmouth snapped, feeling a strange sense of déjà vu as he grabbed her hand and pulled her toward the door to outside. It was time for Miss Sophia Worsley to leave this gambling den, and this time, for good.

The night air cooled his skin but did nothing to calm his thundering heart. The thought—the very image of seeing someone touch Sophia without her consent was insupportable. *What would have happened if he had not decided to go to the gambling den?*

Sophia pulled away, rubbing her wrist pointedly as a reproof. "I said I could manage things by myself," she said coldly, eyes flashing. "I did not need your help. I had everything under control."

"Like hell," Marnmouth repeated, fire in his tone. "And what in God's name were you intending to do, pray, if I had not turned up at that exact moment? Christ alive, Sophia—"

Was that a look of pleasure as he said her name, or had he imagined it?

It was gone before he could say anything. Sophia turned and started walking away.

"Oh no, you don't," muttered Marnmouth. It took only three of his strides before he was right at her side again.

"I had a plan," she said stiffly without looking at him.

It was impossible not to laugh, and so he did. "A plan? God give me strength. What did it involve—shouting or merely struggling?"

She at least had the grace to blush. "That is none of your concern."

She was correct in a way, but Marnmouth could not accept it. *She was his concern—at least, he was concerned for her, and that amounted to the same thing.*

Not just concerned, but utterly captivated.

"A young lady should not be going to places like that," he said in a chastising tone.

He was not surprised when she laughed. "I am not just any young lady, and I will go where I please."

Marnmouth nodded. "I can see that. Do you have any idea where you are going?"

Sophia stopped. It was only then that Marnmouth could see the color in her cheeks, the brightness of her eyes, suggesting tears only just held back, and the quiver of her lip. She had been genuinely afraid, perhaps for her life. *Why could she not just admit that, thank him for his rescue?*

"No," she admitted quietly. "No, I was just walking."

Something softened in Marnmouth's heart. His anger came from fear—fear for her. But she was safe, and she would hardly thank him for preaching at her.

"Sophia—Miss Worsley, I mean," he corrected hastily. "Do your parents know you are out here?"

It was the wrong thing to say.

Firing up again, Sophia snapped, "My parents do not know half the things I get up to because I am old enough to care for myself. I don't need a nursemaid looking after me!"

"Well, I am no nursemaid!" Marnmouth snapped back. It was infuriating having this discussion with her on the pavement, and he tried to keep his voice down. *The last thing they needed was more gossip.* "I would have done the same for any lady in distress!"

"I know, and that is why it doesn't matter to me. If I want heroics, I want them for me, not because of duty."

God, he could not work out this woman. As he looked at her, fiercely staring as though daring him to contradict her, he attempted to unpick what had just occurred.

So did she want him? Did she even like him? It was impossible to tell, and the longer this conversation continued, the more irritated she appeared to become!

Marnmouth laughed and shook his head. "The more I know of you, the more I like you—I would not change you for anything."

Sophia looked curious. "Truthfully? You are in earnest?"

It was, save for her adventure in the Queen of Hearts, the most vulnerable he had seen her. He nodded. "I *would* change the danger you put yourself in."

"Well, as I am nothing to you," she said delicately, "I am not your concern."

Marnmouth swallowed. *How could he put into words the way he felt about Sophia?* If he knew himself, perhaps he could articulate it better.

"I know I am nothing to you, and you are nothing to me, at least in society's eyes," he said in a low voice, "but that does not mean I *feel* nothing for you. I think you feel the same way."

The glare she shot him was worthy of a

queen. "How do you feel about me?"

It was not an unfair question, but Marnmouth hesitated before attempting to respond to such a direct question. "You are...you are precious to me."

Sophia shook her head. "Do not give me that rot. Precious? Like a full purse or a well-shod horse?"

She started walking again. Marnmouth cursed under his breath. *One day he was going to have a conversation with Sophia in which he did not make a fool of himself!*

"No, like—like a piece of music played with passion."

His words, this time, and not his hand, were sufficient to stop her. Sophia turned, her elegant face looking at him as though attempting to discern whether he spoke the truth.

Marnmouth swallowed. *This was his chance.* "Like a poem capturing desperate love. Like a portrait of a loved one accurately made that brings joy to the beholder."

He had never been much good at all this, but for the first time in his life, his words were able to convey something of the stirrings of his heart.

This time, Marnmouth was able to take his time when kissing Sophia Worsley. It was a deep and slow kiss, and he pulled her into his arms as though she belonged there. She resisted, he could feel the tension in her, and he immediately released her.

Sophia was glaring. "You take liberties, sir."

Marnmouth grinned. "You gave them to me, and I want more."

"You cannot have me, so you can just—you can forget that!"

He swallowed. Outside someone's house was not the place to have this discussion. He needed to get her home safely. Then, at least, he could attempt to woo her.

"Let me walk you home," he said aloud, "so I know you are home safely."

He should have known something was up when she turned to the door behind her and smiled broadly. "Well, what do you know? I am at home. It looks as though I know my way about London, after all."

Sophia had shut the door in his face before he could say anything more, and he leaned against it, unable to comprehend what had just occurred.

What had he got himself involved in? Whatever it was, he was not going to allow her to have the last word. Not again.

"Miss Worsley," he yelled, banging on the door with his fist.

As he predicted, it opened within seconds.

"What do you think you are doing?" Sophia hissed, her hair already down past her shoulders, pins removed. "You will wake my parents!"

Marnmouth swallowed. If he had thought

her enticing before, it was nothing to seeing her like this, pelisse removed, hair let down for the evening.

"Looks like you will have to let me in, then," he said with a grin. "Otherwise, I shall just stay out here, knocking on your door."

Sophia bit her lip. She was obviously considering the lesser of two evils, and though it prickled Marnmouth's pride, he was relieved to see she eventually opened the door a little further, albeit with awful grace.

He smiled. "Thank you, Miss Worsley."

The hallway was silent, and its stillness made him wonder what on earth was he doing. Gone were the days when he crept into ladies' bedchambers without their parents' knowledge, and if he knew Miss Worsley—and he was starting to—he should not be aspiring to such a feat this evening.

"This way."

Her voice was a mere whisper, but he followed her and found himself in a beautifully proportioned drawing room with the remnants of a fire still in the grate.

"Well, this is what you wanted," Sophia said, throwing herself on a sofa. "What now?"

Marnmouth whispered, "Will your parents not hear?"

She shook her head. "No, their bedchambers are on the other side of the house. Above is my own—and do not say a thing about it, Marnmouth, or I shall get very irritated with you."

He grinned. "My name is Philip."

"And mine is Sophia, and yet you will call me Miss Worsley, and I will call you Marnmouth," she said smartly, but there was a hint of a smile. "So. What did you intend once you had stormed the barricades?"

If Marnmouth was honest with himself, he had no idea. It had been a reckless hope to be allowed entrance into the Worsley home, and now he was here…

Well, he knew what he wanted to do.

"You know, you are so unlike the other gentlemen I meet," said Sophia lazily.

Marnmouth raised an eyebrow. "How so?"

She looked him up and down carefully before she continued, and he felt a prickle of discomfort settle on the back of his neck.

"Well, most of the time they are either married and so dull, speaking of nothing but their wife or their horses, the latter with more interest—or if they are unmarried," Sophia continued with a smile, "they think of nothing but to flatter me. You are unmarried. Where is my flattery?"

She really was something special, Marnmouth thought. There was something about her that allowed his tongue to loosen in a way it never did with others.

"I do not believe flattery works on you," he said calmly.

"And why not?"

"Because you are unmarried," Marnmouth said with a grin. "If it did work, you would be. Besides, I find it more refreshing to speak truth rather than seek to entertain. Mere entertainment is never usually interesting enough to capture the attention for five minutes, but speaking from the heart…now that is the conversation I seek."

Sophia's smile was the first true one he had seen, melting away her chilly manners.

"That sounds like something you were taught as a child," she said slowly.

Marnmouth laughed, then glanced about in concern. *He must remember the Worsleys were upstairs, utterly unaware an earl was flirting with their daughter below.*

"Beaten into me, more like," he said with a grin. "Like all good boys with titles coming to them, one has to force the truth into them, in case it seeps out of their ears."

He had not expected a reaction to his words, but Sophia sat up and looked genuinely concerned. "I think it barbaric, the way children are beaten for naught but being children."

"I have never really thought about it," Marnmouth said honestly. "I certainly hope my own children are not beaten, for…"

His voice trailed away. *Damn.* He had not

intended to say that. *Something about Sophia drew confidences from him, and he had revealed...damn and blast.*

Sophia rolled her eyes. "You think I am surprised? You are an unmarried gentleman of advanced years—"

"Steady there!"

"—and I am sure you have enjoyed plenty of dalliances over the years," continued Sophia, unruffled. "I would have been surprised if you did not have some illegitimate children running about somewhere. Not in London, I am sure."

Marnmouth shook his head in wonder. "You know, your honesty is refreshing."

Her eyes sparkled. "Let us see whether you can match me."

He swallowed. This had not been his intention. When he wooed women—not that it happened often—he rarely revealed he had got several other women with child.

But Sophia was not any woman. She was a spark in the darkness of society.

This time, however, it was not merely for her person; it was her personality that drew him in. *When had he last had a conversation with anyone this open, this honest—this freeing?*

"I have three daughters," he said with a wry smile. "All various ages, the youngest is six. They live in the country. They live together, actually. Two have the same mother. I see them as often as I can."

"And are you a doting parent?"

Her question was not sarcastic; he could see. She genuinely wanted to know.

"I...I do not think I am, in truth," Marnmouth found himself saying. *God's teeth, how was she able to drag the truth from him?* "I certainly love them in my own way. They are all of my blood, and so I will care for them as best I can for the rest of their lives. But I share no bond with their mothers, and so it cannot be like the love I received from my parents."

Sophia tucked her feet underneath her. "Your parents?"

Marnmouth nodded. "I was fortunate, I believe. Kind, loving, more present than most parents in that time. I may not be elderly, Sophia, but I am certainly older than you, and things were different then."

She rolled her eyes. "Age is immaterial if it comes with true character. Besides, I think my parents follow your own—I am barely permitted my own thoughts each day. At times, I believe they would prefer me to just climb up into an ivory tower and be done with it."

"And would you?"

Sophia smiled. "What do you think?"

"I think you are the most fascinating woman I have ever met," Marnmouth found himself saying. "And I think we would be excellent parents."

Her face froze, and so did his. *Where in God's name had that come from?*

"'Tis getting late," said Sophia softly as she glanced at the clock. "You had better go if I am to get my beauty sleep."

Marnmouth nodded. Perhaps it was best if he simply did not open his mouth for the rest of the time he was with her. *What had possessed him to say such a thing!*

He was standing in the doorway before he knew it, and Sophia had taken his hand.

"Thank you for your wild and unexpected visit," she said quietly, kissing his palm before she released it. "You must come again."

Marnmouth knew what she wanted—could see it in the dark blue of her eyes. He stepped forward, crushed her to him, and kissed her. His mouth ravished her lips until they parted, and he delved in, teasing her until he finally let her go.

They stood there, breathless, knowing something had passed between them that could never be taken back.

"As I said," Sophia said breathlessly. "You must come again."

CHAPTER SEVEN

SOPHIA PICKED UP the nearest book on the shelf in the bookshop and sighed. A puff of dust rose, and she coughed, shaking her head.

Only now, her mother had put her foot down and forbidden her from wearing breeches in public. Gowns were uncomfortable. Her skirts got caught on things, flapped about most irritatingly in a breeze, and she could not move about as freely. *It was maddening.*

One day, she was sure, ladies would wear them freely. *But not today.*

The book she had picked up had a beautiful leather binding and a swirling gold title—so swirling, in fact, she could not make it out. She opened up the book and attempted to take in the first page.

"—oh yes, our daughter Sophia is a fine lady, we are very pleased with her, very pleased indeed," came her mother's words from the other side of the bookshop. "You know, it was only the other day the Earl of Marnmouth called upon her, a very amiable gentleman, I am sure you have heard of him even if you have not made his acquaintance..."

It was no good. She could not concentrate with her mother's words loud enough to ensure everyone else in the bookshop knew that her daughter—yes, *her* daughter—had been visited by an earl.

Sophia had been forced to tell her parents when they found his damned pocketbook on the sofa. It must have fallen out of his greatcoat when he had sat down.

Sophia bit her lip. *She had promised herself no more nonsense, but it was challenging when a gentleman like Philip Egerton had looked at her like that.*

Her parents had been delighted. An earl, see their daughter home?

It was everything they could have wished for.

Sophia was no fool. She knew what assumptions they had made, and it had been difficult preventing her father from inviting him to dinner.

Marnmouth was hers. Her own. She did not know what she wanted to do with him yet, but until she did, she needed to keep her parents as far away from him as possible.

"Engagement! My word, no, the earl has not moved that quick—oh. I see what you mean. No, that engagement did not come to anything…no, nor the one before that. How is your daughter, Mrs. Chesworth? I hear she will have some news to share with the world soon?"

Sophia closed her eyes. The embarrassment in her mother's tone was painful to hear.

Her daughter's past was a source of discomfort. How like Mrs. Chesworth, the woman who loved gossip, to pry. And if Mrs. Chesworth was told the earl was paying attention to Miss Worsley, it would not be long before the whole world knew.

Placing the book back on the shelf and walking down the row, Sophia put some distance between herself and her mother.

The bookshop had been discovered by her mother last year, and they frequented it at least once a week. Sophia brushed her fingers against the leather spines of many books as she passed. New books every month—it was heavenly—*anything to distract her from reality.*

They were not sufficient when the bookshop door opened, and Philip walked in.

She would fade into the background of the shelves.

Every instant since he had left her home two days ago—*two long days*—her thoughts had trickled over to him, no matter what she did.

This was entirely new to her. Even Jacob, to whom she had been engaged for over a year, had not sparked such…interest. *His kisses had never felt like Philip's. Robert had never kissed her at all.*

Sophia watched as the earl walked to the counter, evidently inquiring after a specific book.

Even in the dark and the quiet of the bookshelves where she could remain unseen, Sophia worried he would spot her. What would she do then? Worse, what would her mother do if she realized who he was?

Her whole body came alive when he touched her. *Just a simple touch on her shoulder, around her waist, his lips on hers…*

Sophia shivered. *This was madness.* She had made a solemn promise to leave matrimony behind, and if she could not trust her own promises, where did that leave her?

She was not going to allow herself to think like that. Not about him.

Philip was talking animatedly to the bookseller, and there was laughter and a handshake in their conversation. *Well, that tore it,* Sophia thought wryly. She would never be able to come back here again. This was obviously the Earl of Marnmouth's bookseller.

She had not been back to the Queen of Hearts either. Her near-miss last week was enough to quell any interest. *If Philip had not been there to rescue her…*

Sophia picked up the nearest book and buried her nose in it. And she had not avoided him by refusing to attend Lady Romeril's; that had been complete coincidence. She was still furious at the older woman for her involvement in her failed engagement to Jacob.

The fact that she had received a short note from Philip—*Marnmouth, Marnmouth!*—saying that he would be there had naught to do with it.

She was starting to desire his company to such an extent she would not control herself in public. She could not risk seeing him. Never before had she mistrusted herself.

She certainly did not trust him.

Her decision to linger in the shadows of the bookshelves almost worked. As Philip turned away from the counter, his business completed, he strode down the main walkway but then glanced to his right—directly where she was standing. A bright smile grew across his face.

Sophia felt her cheeks flush. She should not have kissed him.

"As I said, you must come again."

That was simply not what ladies did.

"Why, hello there, Miss Worsley," said Philip with a smile as he leaned on the bookshelf between them. There was a gap just large enough to look through. "I can see you are enjoying one of the most scandalous and lascivious poets of our times."

"Wh-What?" Sophia felt heat pour into her cheeks. *What on earth did he mean?*

Philip did not reply but looked pointedly at her hands. Sophia looked down at the book she had grabbed without paying any heed and saw, to her shock, it was Lord Byron's latest poetry collection.

"I did not even notice," she said with typical bluntness.

It did nothing to dissuade him. "Too distracted by my presence?"

Sophia swallowed. *If her mother even guessed with whom she was speaking…*

"He is a rebellious poet, to be sure, but I think there is elegance in his art," she managed with enough nonchalance for a casual observer to think they did not know each other.

Philip walked around the shelves and appeared in her narrow walkway. There was no bookshelf to protect her now.

He picked out a book yet did not look away as he said, "A rebel poet, you say?"

Emboldened, Sophia smiled. "Yes, although I would say you are the biggest rebel in society at present."

Her words made him laugh. "Other than you?"

Sophia looked over to see whether her mother had realized her daughter was speaking to a well-dressed gentleman and in public.

Yes, Mrs. Worsley would have a fit if she thought her daughter could become a countess, for that was the only conclusion for her matrimony-bent mind.

An earl. Robert had been nothing, and Jacob merely wealthy. What she and Mr. Worsley would do to have an earl as a son-in-law!

But Sophia could see her mother was still in conversation with Mrs. Chesworth.

Turning her attention once more to Philip, she said tartly, "You may not have noticed—I believe you to be too impressed by my presence to think clearly—but you have just picked up a book on the finer points of embroidery."

She giggled as Philip's smile disappeared, and he looked down in surprise at the book on military history.

"Dear me, you are not paying attention," she said with a smile.

He returned it to its shelf, and there was something playful mixed with his seriousness. He was so different from the cavorting gentlemen she was surrounded with. No one in her acquaintance matched him.

"I only picked it up to have the excuse to talk to you."

Sophia's heartbeat quickened. This was another strange and yet wonderful thing about Philip. She always spoke her mind, was famous for her inability to prevent it.

But him? He was an earl, a gentleman. It was part of his place in society to flatter, to smile, to always impress. But he was just as frank as her.

"Walk with me."

Sophia blinked. *He could not have said what she thought he said.* "I beg your pardon?"

Philip jerked his head toward the bookshop door.

Sophia swallowed and again glanced at her mother. Mrs. Worsley had, by the looks of it, finally managed to avoid the topic of daughters and was now speaking animatedly with her friend about the latest Mrs. Radcliffe novel.

What was a lady to do? Her heart begged her to accept Philip's suggestion. A walk in the autumn sunshine in London could not be missed, and with him? It was tantalizing. *But leaving her mother without saying a word, without giving any indication where she was going?*

It would cause nothing but panic and upset.

Sometimes being an only child, let alone the only daughter, was a burden.

"Give me one minute," she said quietly, placing the Byron poetry book back.

"Mother," she said quietly, earning the irate look of Mrs. Chesworth. "Mother, I will see you at home later. I am leaving to…to go on a walk with this gentleman."

Her mother immediately peeked over her shoulder, and Sophia could tell by the broad smile that appeared on her face that she was pleased.

What was not to like? There, behind her daughter, stood a tall, handsome, and well-dressed man.

"Well, that is wonderful," effused Mrs. Worsley quite predictably. "Now, take care not to mention a few topics I know I do not need to spell out to you. Make sure your shawl is tucked close around your neck. Do not—"

"Thank you, Mother," said Sophia hastily to stem the flow of suggestions. "Do not get too excited. I am not going to marry him."

She regretted the words as soon as they were spoken. Her mother flushed, and Mrs. Chesworth grinned triumphantly.

But there was nothing else she could say, and so she turned on her heels and walked toward Philip, who was waiting by the door.

"Come on then," she said, frustrated with her short temper.

A brisk autumnal breeze caught her shawl, just as her mother had predicted, and she grabbed it and tucked it into her pelisse.

Turning to Philip, she saw he looked almost disappointed.

"You said that very decidedly."

Sophia was unsure what he was talking about, and then she laughed. "Yes, I did. Well, that is not what we intend to do today, is it—get wed?"

She said it as lightly as she could and wondered just how much Philip already knew. The gossip of London and Bath spread quickly, it was true, but there were a few Worsleys in society. While her parents had only had one child, she had several cousins of a similar age.

Perhaps he would not tie together the lady who had been jilted twice together with herself?

As they turned a corner, Philip said delicately, "I...well, I know about yourself and Jacob Beauvale, the cad."

The streets of London absolutely teemed as people were drawn from their fires thanks to a bright but blustery day. It was all she could do not to be separated from him on the busy pavement, but she restrained from reaching out and taking his arm.

Taking a deep breath, she said, "No, I cannot, in all honesty, permit him to be described as a cad. He never told me he cared for me, and by all accounts, he is happy with his new wife. I...I cannot begrudge that."

It took great control to speak these words calmly, and she found to her surprise that for the first time, she actually meant them.

Jacob had not touched her heart so deeply that she would ever describe herself as in love with him, but he had hurt her. Now the pain was gone. She had finally put their broken engagement behind her.

Sophia laughed awkwardly. "Though I will admit, at the time, I did not see it that way."

She restrained herself from admitting she had

attempted to blackmail Jacob into marrying her. It had come from a dark place within her. She had never believed it possible that desperation to force him to follow through on his promises would make her do such a thing.

Thank goodness he was braver than she. He was loyal to his new wife, at least.

"Does that lady know you?"

Startled from her reverie, Sophia looked up to see where Philip had indicated with a nod of his head.

Priscilla Seton—well, Priscilla Seton as was. She was the Duchess of Orrinshire now, walking down the street staring curiously at the two of them.

They were acquaintances of a sort. Well, they were both acquaintances of Harry, and that had thrust them into the same gatherings in the country.

If she knew that look, it would not be long before all the gossips in London, and some in Bath, too, would know all about her unchaperoned walk with the Earl of Marnmouth.

Sophia sighed. "Is nothing sacred? Can nothing be kept secret? Is so innocent a walk through the streets of London to be examined? 'Tis hardly as though I am your mistress."

She had intended her final words to be full of levity, but as she glanced at Philip, she saw he was smiling in an all-too knowing way.

"What?"

Philip laughed. "Well, 'tis just interesting that you should mention… I am actually in the market for a wife, you know."

It was a good jest and well made.

Sophia laughed along with him. "Oh, you are? And what is she like, the woman you seek to be your wife? Wealthy, I suppose, and well connected."

She would be mistress of herself. She would prevent any bitterness from seeping in.

"Not especially, no," Philip said airily as they stepped around a corner. "No, the woman I seek to be my wife has to be far more interesting than wealthy. A woman who knows her own mind. Who speaks first because she does not censor herself. One with a strong understanding of herself, who does what she wishes because she wishes it."

Sophia's eyes were downcast. *Was it wishful thinking he was describing her?*

"And in breeches as much as possible," came his teasing voice.

Sophia grinned despite herself as she nudged him. "Not fair Philip—Marnmouth."

"Not so funny now, it is?" he said with a grin. "I have never lied to you, Sophia. You could be my wife, if you wish it."

His teasing words were ridiculous, Sophia knew, but a small part of her wondered whether he would one day say those words to her in earnest.

Could she marry an earl? Nonsense, she thought decidedly. *Remember, Sophia, you have sworn off matrimony.*

There did not seem to be any particular place they were going, just a wandering meander that took them through the center of London.

"Not so bold now, are you?"

Sophia swallowed and looked up into Philip's dark eyes. She needed to hold her own in this, but it was getting more difficult. *She liked him.* He made her feel…

"I am not the only one with a past," she said quietly. "I know all about you, too. Emma Tilbury, for example."

Philip fell silent until they crossed the street. Then he said in a low voice, "I cannot defend myself. I have nothing to defend. You know of my daughters, there is no reason you should not know…I had a mistress, her name was Emma Tilbury, and she was my mistress for a long time. She is my mistress no longer."

Sophia bit her lip. *What did she think she was doing, having this conversation with a gentleman?* Why was it that she was only able to spend ten minutes in Philip's company before secrets and truths started to pour from both their lips, no matter what they did?

"We should start back toward my home," she

said aloud with a bright smile. "My mother will start to wonder—start to assume things."

Why was it that Philip could laugh so easily? "Your mother will be hoping I have made you an offer by now! Yes, I agree, homeward bound."

Sophia sighed. "That is not what—that is not what this is."

Philip stopped and looked curious. "What is this?"

"I do not know," she breathed.

Instead of a sardonic grin, Philip was looking serious. A rush of warmth flew through her as he took her hand.

"Well," he said quietly, "until we know, let's keep walking. Come, your home is this way, I think."

Without asking her permission, he tucked her arm into his, and they began to walk.

Was there greater happiness than this? Walking arm in arm with Philip?

"Have you ever actually read anything by Byron?"

Sophia grinned. "More than you have read anything on embroidery."

CHAPTER EIGHT

Philip watched the dancers move to the lilting music and sighed. His boredom had been replaced with a longing that simply could not be fulfilled—to spend every moment with Miss Sophia Worsley.

True, he had never been bored with Emma—but Sophia was something different.

A smile graced his face as he recalled their London walk just a few days earlier.

The dance finished, the couples bowing and curtseying and applauding the musicians. *No, Sophia did something strange to him, and he could not be held accountable for it.*

"What is the joke?"

Philip started, forgetting he was standing in a group. Miss Isabella Lymington was frowning, and there were muffled giggles from her sisters and a wry smile from Larnwick.

Well, that would teach him. Thinking of Sophia

completely distracted his attention.

"What?" he said before he could get his thoughts together.

Miss Olivia smiled as Miss Isabella Lymington, the elder twin, shook her head. "It does not matter."

Philip could see they were piqued, and it was no surprise why. The chit of a girl, Olivia Lymington, had been throwing herself at him for the entirety of the Larnwick ball.

It must be difficult, he thought to himself. *One's twin, a literal reflection of yourself, about to marry a gentleman with power, consequence, title, and wealth. And you? Just waiting in the wings.*

"What an excellent set of musicians," the duke's betrothed, Isabella, said with a smile. "Always the best for you, Larnwick, clearly."

Perhaps it was because the Lymingtons were from trade, though he was rarely that prejudiced. But they had done their daughters a great disservice, in his opinion, readying them for a life that did not suit them.

One could buy titles, up to a point. But one could not purchase good breeding.

"Thank you, my dear," Larnwick said in a stiff voice. *No love lost there.* "The best musicians for the Larnwick ball, as there always has been and always will."

The conversation moved on as some of the younger Lymington girls joined in, but Philip did not bother to follow it.

What was the point? It was difficult to concentrate on anything these days. Just a few days ago, he had been with Miss Sophia Worsley.

A smile crept across his face. *Yes, she was what he wanted.* He could not put his finger on why. What had he once said?

"Sometimes, a mistress just cannot fulfill all you need. You think she can, and you welcome her to your bed and your life with that intention. But she is not enough. You need a wife for that."

"—later, Marnmouth."

Philip blinked. Larnwick was bowing with his betrothed on his arm and departed with all of his future sisters-in-law.

Not quite all of them.

"Is it not exciting, the Larnwick ball?" said Olivia with a smile. "Why, I do believe that my future brother-in-law has held this ball specifically for my sister, a great honor, I am sure."

Philip grunted. *The less encouragement he could give to Miss Olivia, the better.*

"As far as I know, the duke rarely comes down to London," continued the young lady, "and when he does, the best and brightest of society is here."

He nodded but cast a look about the place and thought privately that, though it was a good smattering of the best, the brightest certainly was not here.

Sophia was not here.

This is foolishness, man! Philip scolded himself as he watched a new set of dancers forming, musicians readying themselves for another piece. He had forbidden himself from thinking of her! *She cannot be the only thing on his mind, can she?*

He grinned despite himself. *Perhaps she was.*

He should have asked Larnwick to invite her. He almost had, but Philip had restrained himself. Requesting an invitation for a lady to another gentleman's ball was not a wise idea.

Besides, the Worsleys might already have been invited. But the night was moving on, and he had seen neither hide nor hair of Sophia or her mother. Her father could be here alone, he supposed, but he had no clue what he looked like.

The Devonshires passed, and he nodded. Montague Cavendish, Duke of Devonshire, completely ignored him, but Philip was not resentful. The holder of one of the most prestigious titles in the land could not be expected to bow and scrape to an earl—though it was a little galling, his lands being in Devonshire.

And there were the Chesters. Chester nodded to Philip, who returned the courtesy There were plenty of people he recognized, but as his gaze swept across them, he did not catch the look of the person he wished to see.

That was foolish. She had made it clear she was not looking to make a match with him.

"Do not get too excited, I am not going to marry him."

But then she was so wild, his Sophia, so rebellious. The memory of those breeches soared back into his mind, and he could not help but laugh.

There truly was no one quite like Sophia.

He had once believed that of Emma Tilbury. He had not considered her equal in beauty or wit had existed, and over the years, that belief had stayed strong, until…

Until it had disappeared. Was this just a passing fancy? An obsession? If Sophia had offered herself to him from the very beginning, would he be this desperate for her company?

A giggle—so false and so coquettish it ground his very soul.

Philip blinked to see Miss Lymington still before him. *Dear God, did she believe he had been listening to her all this time?*

"I know!" she said with a further giggle. "And yet I told him, sir, I am worth thirty thousand pounds! I am hardly like to be seen in company such as yours!"

She laughed again, but Philip did not. *Goodness, she could not be this dim, could she? Was it possible?*

"Yes, indeed," he said blandly. "And what did he—this…this gentleman you speak of—say to you?"

The fan held flirtatiously dropped to her side, and Miss Lymington's face fell. Gone was her simple smile, and instead, there was a fury barely controlled.

"Why does everyone think I am a fool?" she asked directly, no flattery or whining in her voice. "Yes, my twin sister is engaged to a duke, but I am still flesh and blood and deserve to be treated with respect."

Without another word, she walked away.

Philip blinked. He had not imagined such bluntness could exist under such a showy hairstyle, and in truth, he felt ashamed, but he had only ignored her for five minutes. Perhaps she was looked over for her sister more times than she cared to recollect.

He looked in the direction where Miss Lymington had wandered off. *Would it be best if he followed her and attempted to make amends?*

His good intentions were utterly lost, however, when a completely different lady moved into his line of sight, and it was not Miss Lymington but Miss Worsley and what must be her parents. It was certainly her mother, looking very elegant in a gown without any of the fripperies that ladies of her age wore. Sophia, too, was dressed in a lovely gown, though Philip found himself disappointed she was not wearing breeches.

But the gown showed off her figure in almost

as pretty a way as the breeches had, and her parents were watching her closely—very closely, now Philip came to think about it. Evidently, they wished to ensure their daughter only spoke with the right sort of people.

He could not help but smile. *Parents.* So predictable, so wonderfully dependable. After all, the Earl of Marnmouth was well-known for his womanizing or at least had done until a few years ago. Though if Mrs. Worsley's actions were anything to go by, she would welcome his advances to their daughter.

If only Sophia could welcome them just as much.

A desire to speak with Sophia overwhelmed him. Never before had he backed down from the desire to speak to a lady, but this? This was the first time in his memory that he had ever wished to do so for honorable reasons.

Walking slowly around the edge of the ballroom, gently pushing his way through the clusters of people who had bunched up together because of the dancers, Philip felt his heart quicken.

"Marnmouth!"

Philip blinked to find Braedon before him. "Braedon?"

The viscount took him firmly by the hand. "Excellent to see you, old boy—I had not realized you were invited!"

A smile appeared on Philip's face as he tried

to extricate himself, not just from the handshake but from the conversation.

Damn it all to Hell! Just when the Worsleys arrived, he had the misfortune—*no, he should not be so cruel*—the chance to run into Braedon. Now the Worsleys were speaking to an elderly couple he did not recognize, and he was stuck with...

"—so I thought I would come to you," said Braedon, a strange look on his face. *Was that nerves?* "I would not act without your approval, of course, and so when I saw you were here...but you do not speak. Emma told me that it would not do to approach you. I have offended you. I ought not to have spoken."

"What? No, no, not at all," said Philip hastily, finally pulling his hand away. *Emma? Emma who?* "No, you do as you will, Braedon, you know I would never stand in the way of—your decisions are your own."

Whatever it was the man had asked, he now looked delighted. "I knew how it would be! Thank you, your lordship, thank you!"

Braedon disappeared into the crowd, leaving Philip lost. *Emma? Not Tilbury, surely; she and Braedon hardly knew each other. Ought not to have spoken? What had the man been blabbering about?*

But he could not think of that, not now. The elderly couple talking with the Worsleys bowed and moved away. This was his chance.

Sophia's eyes widened as she saw him approaching, and Philip ignored the gentle shake of her head.

"Good evening," he said cheerfully, bowing low. "I know 'tis a terrible breach of etiquette, but after being introduced to your charming daughter at another gathering by the Duchess of Devonshire, I am sure you would not mind me making myself known to you. Philip Egerton, Earl of Marnmouth, at your service."

The second bow was probably a bit much, but Philip could not help himself. It was a dreadful break of etiquette to simply introduce himself. Yet he was an earl. That usually greased the wheels of society, and as he rose from his bow, he saw with a smile he was right.

Mrs. Worsley was nudging her husband and had muttered something in his ear. Philip caught nothing but "bookshop."

"My lord, we are honored," said Mr. Worsley hastily, dropping into a bow.

Philip glanced at Sophia, who was shooting daggers at him. It could not be clearer she had no desire for him to be acquainted with her parents, and he cast her a grin before turning back to the Worsleys.

Well, perhaps it was time to write some of his own rules. They had done everything by her book to date. It was time for a little fun.

"Mr. Worsley," he began courteously. "I wonder whether you would do me the great honor of giving me your permission to stand with your daughter in the next dance. Her honor, of course, will be protected and safe at all times. I merely wish for the joy of her company."

Had he laid it on a little thick? Apparently not. It was clear they could not be happier at the idea. Mrs. Worsley pushed Sophia forward.

"Yes, of course," Mr. Worsley eagerly said. "Sophia would be happy to."

"Sophia would not be happy to," Sophia started to say, but she halted as a particularly large nudge hit her ribs. With a sigh, she said, "Lead on, MacDuff."

Philip grinned as he took her hand. "Did you know Lord MacDuff was a real person? Yes, from a good while ago. I think he stabbed Macbeth in the end."

"I will stab you in a minute," Sophia hissed. "What do you—"

She was forced to halt her words as they bowed and curtseyed to those on either side of them in the set, and Philip wondered whether he had made a grave error as he released her hand.

Sophia's glaring caused something hot and delicious to stir in his loins. *No, no mistake. If he played his cards right, this could actually lead to something rather wonderful.*

"You should have asked me, not my father."

Philip grinned. "You would have said no."

The musicians struck up, and the dance

began. Philip walked toward her and bowed, followed shortly by Sophia, who stepped forward and curtseyed.

And that was it—that was the moment. Something sparked in Philip that was totally new, something he had never known before. He wanted her, true, but he had wanted plenty of other ladies in his time. He had got most of them, too.

This was different. What he felt as they twisted and twirled around each other was…

Well, there was no name for this.

As they joined hands as the dance demanded, both he and Sophia gasped. Even through their gloves, that touch was electric. Their eyes said enough. Sophia's were unusually dark and full of passion, and Philip was sure it would be visible to all that something monumental had occurred between them.

The dance was over too quickly. Philip felt it had hardly begun when the musicians were playing their final note, and applause was ringing out from around them. He felt slightly drunk; there was no other word for it.

What had just happened? Once again, in Sophia's presence, he was utterly wordless, unable to describe what was happening.

When he had first seen her—but no, he had barely taken her in at Beauvale's wedding. At Almack's, when he had approached her for a little flirtation, he had not seriously thought about her. He had not been looking for a mistress. He had certainly not been looking for a wife.

But he had spoken the truth that day on the streets of London when he had jested about the perfect woman for him. Sophia fitted every requirement.

And at this moment, he was just standing here like a fool! Sophia was not the only person peering at him with concern.

"I-I thought…well, if, if, if you want to…" Philip's voice trailed away, and then he coughed. *Get a grip, man!* "Another dance?"

Sophia shook her head as she approached him. "I cannot."

She could not? Was that all she was going to say to him, after experiencing such a moment of connection, after discovering he…

"Why not?" he said, attempting to keep the anger from his voice.

"Because, O titled one, some of us have to work to keep our reputation," Sophia said with a sardonic smile. She reached out to squeeze his arm. "I have to circulate. I cannot simply dance with one gentleman all night, think of the scandal!"

The roll of her eyes calmed his frantically beating heart.

"In that case, let us circulate together. After all," he said quietly, "this entire evening will be a waste if I cannot spend it with you."

Every word he spoke was true. By God, she drew him in like a courtesan, and yet there was innocence even more intoxicating.

Sophia smiled. "I am afraid not, your lordship."

Irritation flickered at Philip's soul. "Hell, why not?"

"Well, I am still just about marriageable, am I not?" Sophia looked through her lashes in that way he was certain she knew made him want to rip all her clothes off. "I have to ensure that everyone knows it. Ah, look. My parents wish to introduce me to Viscount Braedon."

And in a flurry of silk, she was gone.

Philip stood, unable to move. It was as though someone had run him through with a blade. Sophia had rejoined her parents, and there, true to her word, was Braedon. Thankfully, he looked just as discomforted as Sophia. She did not look around.

The sensation of being stabbed with a sword intensified.

Christ alive, but it had finally happened. He had avoided it for so long, a part of him had wondered whether it was even possible.

He was in love. He had fallen in love with Miss Sophia Worsley, and worst of all, now he knew it, he could not live without her.

Sophia was a part of him now, and his life would be incomplete without her. But after all his jesting, how to convince her he was serious?

CHAPTER NINE

SOPHIA STRODE PURPOSEFULLY down the autumnal London street. She pulled her pelisse closer and wondered what on earth had possessed her to think this was a good idea.

It had struck her, the thought, as she had breakfasted with her parents that morning. It was wild, it was *forward*, and it was certainly something her parents would not approve of.

It was perfect.

Taking a deep breath as she turned a corner, Sophia tugged her bonnet a little lower over her face. She was not ashamed—but there would be those who would attempt to shame her, and the fewer people who recognized her, the better.

Now she had started this short journey, only a few London streets over from her parents' home, she was determined to finish it.

She was not exactly calling on him, as such. It would certainly look like that to the casual observer. She had not been invited, and their families were not so intimately acquainted that it was appropriate to simply turn up, as she was doing.

No, not calling on Philip. She was…*ascertaining his wellbeing.*

It was a silly phrase but one which gave her the confidence to keep putting one foot before the other, taking her closer and closer to his residence.

She had not seen him for a week and that was unusual. Every couple of days for weeks they had…encountered one another. It had never been planned—at least, not from her side.

Sophia smiled at the memory of a particularly pleasant walk in Hyde Park seven days ago, the last time she had seen him. He had laughed at her jests, teased her, told her such stories of the world from when he was younger…

Not that she was in any way attached to him. Sophia pushed aside the memory of that heady dance at the Larnwick Ball, unable to explain the rush of emotions the encounter had stirred. She had been careful never to permit Philip to touch her since. He was always tantalizingly out of reach, but she could not risk a loss of control again.

Stepping aside to allow a family to pass on the pavement, she attempted to get a hold of her thoughts.

She had never done anything like this before. Even when she and Jacob had been engaged, and he had gone weeks without seeing either her or her parents, she had not simply turned up outside his door and demanded to see him.

So why was she paying this courtesy, nay this compliment, to a man she...

She swallowed and glanced at the street sign above her. Just one over from Philip's—from the Earl of Marnmouth's residence.

There were only so many places one could meet others, and she had unusually—and to the delight of her parents—attended them all in the preceding week.

But Philip had not attended Almack's, even though she had carefully chosen her favorite gown and made a fuss to claim her mother's lady's maid to prepare her hair. Philip had not been in the bookshop. Not only had Sophia dropped by a few times each day, but to her blushing shame, she had actually inquired of the proprietor whether the Earl of Marnmouth had been in recently. He had not.

No one had seen him. Philip had simply decided not to venture out into society.

It was time to take things into her own hands.

Sophia smiled as she carefully crossed the street, avoiding the carriages. Philip reaching for her hand at the Larnwick Ball, the way her body had reacted to his every touch...

"You should have asked me, not my father."
"You would have said no."

Perhaps there was some ulterior motive. She had never felt more alive than when dancing with him.

That was saying something. After all, how many gentlemen had she danced with in her years in society? Hundreds, probably. Yet despite their affectations, charms, their desire to impress…none had a patch on Philip. None melted her bones, made her…

Made her want to do things that were simply not ladylike.

Even now, when she had not seen him for over a week, the mere thought of him was enough to make her heart start racing as she stepped onto Park Lane, Mayfair.

Sophia swallowed down the panic rising alongside the excitement. This was a rebellious act, to be sure, yet no one could judge her poorly for this…this charitable act.

And then she suddenly found herself standing outside Number Eight, where a large bell hung down to the right of the front door. The metal was cold underneath her fingertips. She had forgotten to wear gloves.

Ignoring the frantic beating of her heart and any possibility she may regret this later, Sophia pulled on the bell and heard the clanging echo inside the building.

Nothing else happened.

Sophia's heart was beating so loudly, she could hear it pulsing in her ears, the hustle and bustle of the street continuing: newspaper boys shouting the latest headlines, food sellers attempting to promote their wares, and the chatter of gentlemen and ladies filling the air.

But the door did not move.

Sophia frowned. No servant was perfect, obviously, but she would have expected far better for the Earl of Marnmouth. *Surely someone should have put down the silver polish or something and come to the door?*

Impetuously, she reached out and rang the doorbell again, knocking on the door for good measure. She may as well have stood silently, for nothing happened.

Heat seared her cheeks as Sophia wondered what was happening. Was it possible that Philip was inside but had instructed his servants not to open the door?

Worse, had he told them to forbid her entrance?

The very thought made her stomach twist. She had teased him a little too much, perhaps. Had she not laughed at his jokes sufficiently?

No, that was not the Philip she knew. He would not take offense to such nonsense. Something was wrong.

Just as Sophia stepped back down onto the street and turned her back, deciding to return home and plot her next course of action from there, a scraping sound echoed in the street.

"Miss—Miss!"

Sophia looked up. A window from the third floor had been pushed open, and a maid was peering out.

"You looking for m'lordship?"

It was all she could do not to blush as Sophia said, "Why—why yes, I am."

The maid nodded. "I thought so. Sorry, Miss, he's gone."

Foreboding washed over Sophia as she pulled her pelisse closer. "What do you mean, gone?"

"House is all shut up, and he's gone to Bath, hasn't he?" said the maid matter-of-factly. "No idea how long, he'll be back when he decides, I suppose. Or he'll stay for the Season. Leastways, I never gets told."

Sophia nodded. "I see. Yes, right, thank you."

The maid disappeared, and the window closed against the chilling breeze as Sophia stood, dumbfounded, on the pavement.

Gone. Gone to Bath, without even a word, a note.

Was it right to feel slighted? There was certainly a bitter sensation twisting in her stomach, and she felt a little lightheaded, although she would be the last person to admit that Philip—*the Earl of Marnmouth, that is*—was the cause.

Why had he not mentioned a Bath visit to her? It would have been simple enough to slip into conversation, just a mention he was going to Bath for the Season.

But then, why would he?

"Do not get too excited, I am not going to marry him."

"I have been jilted before, sir, and have no interest in matrimony. Now go away."

"Well, I am marriageable, am I not? I have to ensure that everyone knows it."

Regret seared her heart at the memory of her words.

He had wished to dance with her, spend more time with her. He had wanted her for…well, things a gentleman was not supposed to do with a lady before marriage.

Did he think her jesting serious? Was he even now in Bath, courting some other young lady because he thought she was uninterested?

The thought pierced her heart, turning her emotional distress into physical pain.

Had she made a terrible mistake?

After two engagements that had not touched her, it was time to admit Philip had broken through the barriers she had set around her heart.

Was it love? Sophia did not know. Whenever she read about love in the poems or romances of the day, or even the classics—Vergil, Ovid—there was joy, yes, but most of love appeared to be pain. *Heartache.*

This was certainly what she was experiencing

now. Robert and Jacob, they had barely stood out from the other gentlemen in society, save for that she was supposed to marry them.

Being jilted had injured her pride more than her soul.

Whatever she felt for Philip made her wretched. Where she had once been whole, something was missing, a part of her heartbroken, and that piece had disappeared from London.

It was in Bath, damn him.

What could she do about it now? Nothing. If Philip had mentioned his plans to depart to Bath for the Season, she could have said something. Persuaded him to stay.

Sophia smiled wryly as she leaned against the railings of Number Eight. *But what would she have said? She surely would not have admitted that she…that she felt…*

And now she could not even write him a letter, that was far too intimate. He had not requested her permission to correspond.

Sophia looked out at the street, full to the brim with people with their own concerns, pains, thoughts. None of them could know her agony, just as she could never predict theirs.

She would have to accept Philip was in Bath.

A mischievous smile crept over her face. Or at least, that was what she would have accepted before she had decided to be rebellious, to not care what society thought. So what was she doing standing here like a fool?

Fifteen minutes was all the time it took for Sophia's quick feet to return her home. The front door closed, and she sighed as warmth started to defrost her bones.

As she swept off her pelisse and bonnet and laid them carefully on the chair by the door, her father stepped into the hallway.

"Ah, Sophia, I had started to wonder where you had got to," he said jovially. "And where have you been this fine morning?"

"Nowhere," said Sophia automatically. She should have known better than to attempt to leave the conversation at that.

Mr. Worsley rolled his eyes in the precise manner of his daughter. "Well, where are you off to next? Your mother has just returned from your favorite bookshop, you know, and has discovered a wonderful—"

"Bath," said Sophia shortly as she started to ascend the staircase.

"A bath? At this time in the morning?"

Sophia halted on the stairs and took a deep breath. *This was going to cause an argument, she just knew it.*

"No, not *a* bath," she said. "Bath, the town. I will depart immediately. I just need to pack."

"Righty ho," said Mr. Worsley absentmindedly, and then Sophia saw his eyes sharpen. "Wait—what? Come down here, Sophia, this is a discussion, not a report!"

It was on the tip of Sophia's tongue to retort she had reached her majority and, as long as she used her income, could do what she wanted—but disobedience was not worth the antagonism it would cause.

Stepping heavily back down the stairs, she said, "What needs discussion?"

Before her father could reply, her mother entered the hallway. "Ah, I thought I heard your voice, Sophia. I hope you enjoyed your walk. And what are you two talking about?"

"Your daughter says she is going to Bath!" Mr. Worsley said, pointing at Sophia, which she thought most unnecessary.

Mrs. Worsley looked supremely uncon-cerned. "Yes, in a few weeks. I must admit I am excited. London is so dirty in the winter, and it is much more pleasant to spend the Season in Bath."

Sophia took a deep breath. She never acted to hurt her parents, not exactly. It was such a shame so much of her life pained them, whether she intended it or not.

"No, not in a few weeks," she said. "Today. Within the hour, if I can manage it."

Turning away from her parents, hoping this decisive tone would reduce any argument, Sophia started walking up the stairs.

Her father was spluttering. "B-But—Sophia, what on earth are you talking—today?"

But her mother was thinking along more practical lines. "Sophia, we cannot possibly spare the carriage for you—not all the way to Bath!"

Sophia had reached the top of the stairs, and after stepping along the corridor, she closed her bedchamber door, blocking out the sound of her parents' apoplectic horror at the idea of their daughter deciding on a whim to travel over a hundred miles!

It took but five minutes to pack a trunk. *After all, how long would she be in Bath? Not long.* Just enough time to find Philip, understand why he had callously abandoned her to the society of London without even a word, and then…

Sophia swallowed as she fastened the buckle of her smallest trunk. She had not thought that far ahead, but she was sure an idea would present itself in time. The most important thing was to get there.

The very idea of being over a hundred miles away from Philip…it tore at her very being. *It was wrong, the world was wrong when they were this far apart, and she was about to make it right.*

"M'lady?"

Her mother's lady's maid, Loughton, poked her head around the door, and the noise of Mr. and Mrs. Worsley's outrage seeped into the room.

"Ah, Loughton," Sophia said smartly. "Please take that trunk downstairs for me."

Pulling a fresh bonnet from its box, she followed the maid downstairs and found her parents almost precisely where she had left them—outraged at the bottom of the stairs.

"What do you think you are doing?" Mrs. Worsley said, wringing her hands.

Sophia bit her lip. It was clear her mother loved her dearly and did not wish her to carry out this plan—but then, she had no choice, really. *She had to be near Philip.*

"No, I see what it is," said her father bitterly. "She has already made a fine spectacle of herself in London, so now she wishes to return to Bath to do the same thing!"

Sophia opened her mouth to retort, but her mother glared at Mr. Worsley so rapidly he looked downcast.

Mrs. Worsley turned to her daughter with an understanding smile. "I am sure you have your reasons for wishing to go to Bath, Sophia, but...well. Everyone there knows about...about Jacob."

Sophia threw up her hands. "Everyone everywhere knows about that!"

It was all she could do to stay calm. *Really, did her parents think she would never return to Bath in case someone recognized her?*

"I am putting my foot down," said Mr. Worsley decidedly as the maid placed Sophia's trunk on the chair by the door and scuttled away from the argument. "You are not going."

Sophia smiled. "I am of age, and I am going."

"Wh-What? You cannot!" spluttered her mother.

"And why on earth not?"

Sophia's question rang out in the hallway, and for once, her parents had no answer. She tied her bonnet on and pulled her pelisse around her.

"I refuse you use of the carriage," her father said quietly. "There, it is decided. Now take your pelisse off and stop being so foolish, Sophia."

But his daughter smiled. "Then, I will take the mail coach."

Within her heart, she knew she needed to be near Philip. She loved him. She had never considered herself likely to fall in love, but here it was. He did not return her affections; he could not if he simply took off to Bath without saying a word. Yet, she had to be near him. It was something she could not understand nor describe.

Every mile that would close the gap would put her soul at ease.

"I will see you in a few weeks," she said aloud, picking up her trunk with difficulty. "I will have the rooms ready for you."

Incoherent words were spluttered behind her, but Sophia had already opened the front door with her trunk under one arm and started walking outside.

This was truly a rebellious thing, far more rebellious than she had done before. *What would Philip say when she arrived in Bath?*

CHAPTER TEN

I T HAD BEEN a busy day, what with reviewing his accounts, receiving letters from his steward, and trying to untangle a few disagreements his tenants had got into in his absence.

Marnmouth. He really should attempt to spend more time there. It was unconscionable that he would spend so much time away from it—and yet, there had never been much to tempt him back.

The Devon town was out of the way, parochial. The latest fashions had last graced the streets of London when he had been a child. There were no concerts, little society… It was no wonder he felt called back to London, to Bath, to society after more than a fortnight in his seat.

Philip yawned, and the candle on his desk fluttered. He had been at this for hours and was surely going to make no more progress with exhaustion in his bones.

Just as Philip rose, there was a knock—slightly muffled as the study was upstairs and near the back of the townhouse, but a knock on the front door.

His acquaintance was not in Bath yet; he was several weeks too early for the Season. It was why he had come now. More progress could be made if he was left undisturbed, although it appeared someone had found him out.

Sighing heavily, Philip strode across the room and opened the door, leaning over the railings just in time to see McCall moving toward the front door. "I will get it, McCall."

The elderly man jumped at the sudden voice of his master and looked around.

Philip smiled as there was another knock with greater urgency. "Up here, man."

The butler raised his gaze. "Ah, your lordship. Are you certain you are happy to answer the door?"

Philip nodded as he descended the stairs and grasped the older man's arm. "You have been of great use to me today, McCall, and I am most grateful. Consider me standing you down for the evening. Go and rest."

The banging at the front door echoed through the hallway as the butler smiled. "Thank you, my lord. I admit, I am tired and will use this time to get a little sleep. Good evening, your lordship."

As McCall shuffled away down the servants' corridor, Philip watched him go. *It really was time to look for a replacement for the old man, perhaps start one of the upper footmen into some training. McCall had served his time.*

Loyalty, that was what Philip prized before all else. Servants could drop plates, miss cleaning under rugs, he did not really care. It was their loyalty he wanted, and when a man like his butler had stayed with him for over thirty years, that deserved reward.

Philip's thoughts were immediately interrupted by the raucous knocking at his front door, and his smile disappeared to be replaced by a frown.

Striding over to the door, he started to mutter. "And what sort of person makes such a racket at this late—"

His voice was utterly silenced as he threw open the door and saw a person he could never have expected to find on his doorstep.

Sophia. She was standing in pelisse and bonnet, a small trunk under her arm, cheeks pink from the cold wind.

Philip's mouth fell open. *Was it possible—had he fallen asleep in his chair in the study, as he dreamt of Miss Sophia Worsley?*

It would not be the first time she had graced his dreams, although typically, she was wearing significantly fewer clothes.

Philip closed his mouth hastily. *This was not possible—Sophia was in London! She could not be here!*

A nervous smile crept over Sophia's face. "Hello."

A response. He needed to respond. It was ridiculous to stand here, staring as though he had never seen a woman before. But his mouth was dry, his throat scratchy, and he was unsure whether he would make himself understood if he even attempted it.

A squalling breeze rushed through them, and finally, a little common sense fell into his brain, something he was in dire need of.

"Sophia—Miss Worsley, you must be freezing," he said. "Come in, please."

Stepping aside to make room for her, Philip tried not to think. *But what was she doing here?*

"Thank you, I am sure," she said quietly, stepping forward.

Damn and blast it, but what was happening? Had Sophia really come—she could not have traveled from London to Bath, and seemingly alone, just to see him…*could she?*

Philip shut the door and, before he turned, attempted to marshal his thoughts. Almost as though his desire to see her had willed her into being, she was in his house.

Philip knew this would tell him whether he was dreaming or not. In those delicious dreams when he removed her pelisse, there was nothing else but pure Sophia...

Sadly, *this* Sophia was wearing a pretty muslin day gown. The pelisse in his hands was warm. *Sophia Worsley was in his house and everyone else in bed.*

No one would ever know she was here. No one would know what he and she—*no. He had to be a gentleman. He would not try to seduce Sophia. Probably.*

Sophia stood there in her gown, trunk beside the door, clearly waiting for him to speak.

Philip smiled. *Finally, the chance to treat Sophia to a little Marnmouth hospitality.* Perhaps this was a blessing in disguise. Whatever reason she was here, he could now spend precious time in her company.

"This way," he managed to articulate, indicating she should step into the next room.

The drawing room fire was warm, and yet the familiar furniture, the wallpaper he knew so well, felt strange now.

Sophia Worsley was here. Like two worlds colliding, a small part of Philip wished he had been forewarned of her arrival. Then he would have had time to...

What? What would he have done differently? He liked his townhouse. Besides, Sophia did not seem to have any qualms with the decoration. To the contrary, she was looking around with wide eyes, obviously impressed with the way he had furnished it.

Philip shook his head. No, he could not think like that. That would get him nowhere. Sophia had been perfectly clear, despite his apparent affections, that she was steering clear of all matrimonial pursuits.

Damn it. Yet those kisses! That dance, the way she had curled into his body for protection when he had saved her from that brute in the Queen of Hearts.

It was enough to turn any man's head. Philip wanted her, wanted her so desperately, but the flavor of that want was still undecided. Yes, he had offered her marriage in a jesting way. But the more he saw of her, the more he wanted her.

First things first. What in God's name was she doing here?

"Please, sit down," he said hastily, realizing he had left Sophia in silence.

She sat on the sofa, nearest the fire. "Thank you."

Philip should have taken a deep breath, attempted to gather his thoughts—but he spoke straight from the heart. "What on earth are you doing here?"

Sadly, his tone did not encourage confidence. "I could ask you the same question!" said Sophia, flaring up.

Philip sat beside her, attempting to keep at

least a few inches between them lest he lose control and just tried to kiss the truth out of her.

"I will admit I am a little astonished," he said. "I had only intended to be in Bath for a few days, and then return to London. Return to you."

That last sentence had slipped out before he could stop it, and it visibly mollified his unexpected guest.

Her voice softened. "I…I still do not understand why you left without telling me."

Philip found relief soared through his heart. *Sophia must care for him, even a little, if she was this upset by his absence.* Why, he had not even considered it worth telling her.

"I wish I had," he said quietly. "But I must say, Sophia, there is getting irritated that someone you are acquainted with has left town, and then there is traveling across the country to tell him so."

With pleasure, he saw her cheeks pink, and her hands clasp together in her lap. *Yes, she felt something for him, he could see that—whether she knew it herself, he was not so sure.*

"Besides," Philip continued, "you once told me you were extremely marriageable and had to circulate society to ensure that all gentlemen knew. I thought you were being wined and dined by others."

He had promised himself that hurt would not seep into his voice, but he failed. It did not seem to matter.

"You were jealous."

Philip swallowed. If he were not careful, this conversation would run away from him, and he would be forced to make an admission he was not yet ready to.

After all, this was his house. She was the one who had turned up on his doorstep.

"Of course not," he said, bluffing. "I was just conscious of what you had asked me to do when we last danced together. To stay away from you."

"Yes, I...I did say that," said Sophia, nodding. "But that does not prevent you from being jealous at the same time. Why did you not say?"

Philip swallowed nervously before he did what he'd been longing for, and captured her in his hungry arms.

There was nothing else like Sophia. Her scent, the feeling of his arms around her waist, the way she moaned as his fingers brushed the nape of her neck...

When the kiss finally ended, Philip looked into her bright eyes and saw the same fear and desire he was sure were in his own.

"You frightened me," Sophia whispered. "Leaving London like that. Leaving me."

Philip smiled. The fear of sharing his emotions evaporated. Sophia had taken the first step, and it was time to do likewise.

"I hate the idea of frightening you. You

frightened me by coming here. I thought something had happened. But why on earth would you feel that?"

Sophia's frown was mocking. "You know why, Philip. Do not play games with me."

Philip's smile broadened. "You—*you* were jealous! You were concerned I had gone off with some mistress, made an assignation in Bath, or left London to meet some woman!"

"Well?" Sophia's eyebrows raised as she examined him. "Hadn't you?"

The temptation to twist the truth, to make himself look more impressive, flashed through Philip's mind, but he pushed it away. No, he would treat her with the honesty and respect she deserved.

"Wait here," he said quietly.

It felt wrong to release Sophia from his embrace, but it would be worth it once he returned—once he had demonstrated his loyalty to her. Philip grabbed two red ledger books from his desk, and within another minute, was back in the drawing room seated beside Sophia.

"There," he said triumphantly, putting the heavy books into her lap.

Sophia laughed, opening the cover of the first one. "What on earth are these?"

"Ledger books. Financial records," explained Philip with a sigh. "Not my favorite chore, to be sure, but it should be done at least once a year, and I did not bother last year."

Her eyes were wide, and so Philip gave a little more detail, feeling odd as he moved his finger down the penciled columns.

"See—here, a list of all my lands around Marnmouth. Devon," he clarified, seeing her confusion. "'Tis much easier to come to Bath for the accounts rather than stay in London. It's much closer, you see. Any questions for my steward reach me at least two days earlier."

He was not entirely sure what response he had expected, but it was not a laugh. Sophia giggled, flicking through the pages with her delicate fingers.

"Is that all?"

Philip shrugged. "I told you it was dull."

Sophia looked relieved, and he was tempted to ask her to stay the night. *By God, but if he could use this joy to get her into his bed…*

No. He promised not to seduce her.

"Stay for supper," he said impetuously, desperate for an excuse to keep her with him.

Evidently, he was not as circumspect as he believed. The look Sophia bestowed on him demonstrated she knew what he really wanted.

"I am afraid I cannot," she said with real regret. "I need to go to my parents' house in Gay Street, ensure it is opened up for them."

"Oh," said Philip. Despite his disappointment, he rallied and said, "They are here, in Bath, then?"

Sophia rolled her eyes in that delightful way he loved. "We were not supposed to be coming to Bath for a few weeks. It is likely we will return to London for a few engagements we have already—but after I decided to—well, they are coming tomorrow."

Before he knew what he was about, Philip said, "Well, you must all come to dinner tomorrow, after they have arrived. They will be exhausted after all their traveling, and I doubt your kitchens will be ready for them. The last thing they will want is a cold meal after such a long journey."

It was an open invitation, and it was politely made—so why did Philip feel as though his life depended on her response?

He watched her hesitate, and his stomach dropped. Would she not even accept an innocent invitation to dine with her parents as chaperones?

"Yes, I am sure they will be delighted," she said finally. "And now I must go, Philip."

The tension between them had not disappeared. It would be safer for her to go. She clearly did not wish to be tempted, and God knew he was.

"Of course," he said, setting the ledgers down and leading her into the hall. "Here, let me."

Holding out her pelisse, Philip allowed himself an embrace as she pulled her arms through it, pulling her back into his chest, his arms around her waist.

Sophia leaned against him, and they stood there. "I really do need to go."

Philip nodded and kissed her neck. "I know."

Sophia laughed as she pulled away. "You are incorrigible, Philip. Until tomorrow."

"Until tomorrow."

After picking up her trunk, she closed the door, leaving Philip standing alone.

What did he think he was doing? Courting Miss Sophia Worsley? After all these years, was he really about to propose marriage?

CHAPTER ELEVEN

"How wonderful this all is!" her mother said. "To think! In Bath a little earlier than we had originally intended, to be sure, but starting the Season early cannot be a concern when prompted by our dear Sophia's attachment to the Earl of—"

"Mother," Sophia interrupted. They had not even arrived at Philip's home in Camden Place, and already her parents were utterly intolerable. "Mother, you are mistaken. There is no attachment between us."

Her father snorted. "No attachment? We were not born yesterday. Sophia, do not treat us as innocents. Don't think we do not know precisely why you stormed here just days ago."

Sophia swallowed. Her anxiety was starting to play havoc with her stomach, and all she wanted to do was keep her mouth shut, but this could not continue.

"No, Father, it was—"

"A tad rebellious, and not something I would typically authorize," Mr. Worsley continued without paying any heed, "I believe it will all work out in the end. Well done, Sophia. You are, I think, to be congratulated."

Sophia rolled her eyes. "You suppose too much! My reason for coming to Bath was not precisely as you imagine. In truth—"

"The Countess of Marnmouth," said her mother dreamily, her eyes looking out of the window as the carriage turned a corner. "What a title!"

Sophia sighed and desisted in her attempts to rein in her parents' suppositions. *Well, what harm would it do, really?* They were too well-bred to speak these assumptions to Philip, weren't they? She would not have to face him with such nonsense, would she?

"Oooh, we are here, we are here!" Mrs. Worsley almost jumped in her seat, making the carriage rock. "Sophia, look, we are here!"

Sophia smiled weakly.

The carriage slowed, and Sophia took a deep breath to steady her nerves.

It was difficult to untangle her emotions raging through her heart. Even now, sitting in the carriage as her father fussed about whether his cravat was straight, she was tempted to return to their rooms.

She was a grown lady, after all, and if she decided to just return home…

Her heart rebelled against her mind.

It was an intoxicating sensation, the realization that one's happiness depended on another. *She did not like it.*

"Come on, Sophia."

"Yes, thank you," she said distractedly as her mother gazed up at the townhouse.

"What a fortunate thing it was that his lordship was able to find himself rooms at *Camden Place*," Mrs. Worsley murmured as Sophia joined her on the pavement. "Such a prestigious address."

Sophia spoke without thinking. "He did not acquire the rooms for the Season, Mother, 'tis his Bath townhouse."

She regretted it as soon as she had spoken, but it was too late.

"What—his *own* townhouse?" Her mother collapsed into rhapsodies on the theme of her intended son-in-law. "My word, what a wealthy and well-placed gentleman—did you hear that, Arthur? His own rooms! Goodness, we shall have to be on our best behavior when—"

"Yes, please," said Sophia hastily, taking her mother's hand and squeezing it with a smile. "Best behavior all around, I think."

Was that a sardonic look her father gave her? It was gone in a moment as he walked up the steps to knock on the door—but as he raised his hand, the door opened.

A liveried footman stood in the doorway. "Ah, Mr. Worsley, Mrs. Worsley, Miss Worsley. You are expected."

He bowed and stepped aside.

Mrs. Worsley squeezed her daughter's hand. "Far more impressive than anything young Beauvale could manage, is it not?"

Sophia closed her eyes for a moment before following her father. *It was too much. What had she been thinking, allowing herself to engage her parents for dinner with Philip?*

It was times like these she had to remember that her parents loved her and wished only good things. They did have this rather strange obsession for marrying her off.

"Ah, Mr. Worsley!"

Her heart skipped a beat. There he was, shaking her father's hand.

"But—now, Miss Worsley, I thought I had been clear with you!" Philip's voice was stern, and Sophia started in surprise. *What on earth had she done wrong now?* "I instructed you to extend my invitation to dine to your parents, and you have brought me your father and someone I presume must be your sister!"

"I declare, your lordship!" giggled Mrs. Worsley.

Philip winked at Sophia as he helped her

mother out of her pelisse, and Sophia could do nothing but shake her head with a wry smile. Perhaps she did not need to be so concerned after all. Perhaps her parents' nonsense and Philip's would mesh perfectly.

"I hear, my lord, my daughter has hunted you out!" said Mr. Worsley.

Philip laughed as he indicated the drawing room. "She has indeed, and I am all too grateful, for it gives me the wonderful excuse to know you all better. Please, come through."

Sophia closed her eyes, took a deep breath, and opened them again as Philip stepped forward with her mother on his arm. *Why was he doing this—it was intolerable!*

All she had to do was survive…*what a few hours, maybe three hours at worst?* Then it would all be over, and her parents would never have to interact with Philip again.

As she stepped into the drawing room, she saw Philip making a huge fuss over her mother, attempting to ascertain if she would be too hot near the fire or too cold if she did not.

Of course, her parents loved him. *How could they not?* He was everything Jacob was—good breeding, elegant manners, wealth—and had all that Jacob had not, such as a title and townhouse in Camden Place, Bath.

But even more than that, he was charming. *He was charming!* And the worst thing was, of course, Philip knew it. There was that knowing grin on his face as he exchanged a joke with Mr. Worsley about the horse races in the last season. *He knew what he was doing.*

"Miss Worsley," he said, turning to her suddenly. "Please do help yourself to a seat while I help your mother to a drink."

Sophia sat in an armchair as she watched with amazement as Philip acted as footman for her parents, waiting on them, pouring them wine, and doing a charming job of it.

Despite herself, Sophia was impressed. She had seen the gruff Philip when he had…not exactly *rescued* her from the Queen of Hearts. She had seen the protective side of him, the irresistible side of him. He had made her laugh, made her furious, and now?

Now he was charm itself. Would this man never cease amazing her?

It was seven o'clock before she knew it, and the dinner gong echoed.

"Now, Mrs. Worsley, you will have to forgive me," said Philip as he rose. "And I beg you will, or I shall be devastated."

"Forgive you, your lordship? I know not what you mean, but I am sure you will be able to explain yourself," said Mrs. Worsley prettily.

Philip sighed theatrically. "'Tis only that I wish I could walk both yourself and your daughter to the table, but I am forced to choose between you—and alas, I admit I would choose the latter. Can you ever forgive me?"

Mrs. Worsley fell into raptures of delight.

As Philip stepped forward to take Sophia's arm, she glared. "Do you not think you are laying it on a bit thick?"

He grinned. "Nothing is too much for your parents."

She laughed despite herself. It was difficult to be irritated with a gentleman who was doing everything to impress those she loved. *Where had this devotion to her joy come from? And why did it make her feel so unbearably happy?*

The dining room had been decorated with such sumptuous attention to detail; Sophia was sure it was Philip's doing. There were sprigs of rosemary all down the table, lending their subtle fragrance to the air. Candles were lit in every possible place, looking glasses placed along the walls making the whole room shimmer. There was even a young gentleman seated in the corner with a violin in his arms in the same livery as the footmen who served them.

"Ah, music!" Mr. Worsley said appreciatively. "Now that is a nice touch, is it not, Sophia?"

Sophia was forced to admit that yes, it was, as Philip helped her to a seat. *Where had all this come from—and more importantly, where was it all going?*

The dinner was delicious. Each course was more fragrant and delectable than the last, and

Sophia was so busy eating that she hardly contributed to the conversation—which was nowhere as near as uncomfortable as she had predicted.

With Philip seated beside her and her father opposite, she watched the two gentlemen jest and laugh over political jokes. It was strangely pleasant to see them converse so happily.

Robert had never met him, and Jacob…*well.* The poor boy had been orphaned at a young age, so perhaps it was not fair to blame him for his complete lack of manners.

And Mrs. Worsley was not ignored. Sophia watched in awe as Philip flattered her in a respectful and yet gentle way.

The last thing she needed was for her parents to get the wrong idea. She was not going to marry Philip, even if he asked her. They had been so approving of Jacob, and Philip was so much more impressive. The debate would be uncomfortable, and she knew what they would ask.

What was wrong with him?

Sophia picked at her dessert as she cast a glance at the gentleman beside her. What *was* wrong with him? Why was she so set against something she desperately longed for?

"Not interested in being a mistress, then. What about a wife?"

Why wouldn't she marry Philip if he decided to ask her seriously?

"No, truly, your lordship?"

"My dear Mrs. Worsley, I wish you would call me Marnmouth, 'tis so much more friendly, do not you think?"

Sophia rolled her eyes. If it was not enough that she had fallen in love with him, now her mother was going to fall in love with him, too!

And it was love. That was why she had to stop herself from saying something foolish like she would marry him. Because Philip now had the ultimate power over her, the power no other gentleman had ever won.

The power to make her truly unhappy.

Was it typical to feel this...well, possessive over a gentleman one had no actual ownership of? *Why did her mind fill with visions of them having this dinner once a week, so her parents could continue to know Philip better, her husband, while she was able to enjoy him alone the rest of the week?*

Heat tinged Sophia's cheeks as she put the vision of that life aside.

"—never seen a boar that large, I tell you," her father was saying, his hands moving wildly as he attempted to describe the hunt to Philip. The younger man caught her eye and winked. "My horse was pretty ragged, but I was certain I could force the old mare into action, so I..."

She was warm, too warm, and she tried to cool herself by taking a sip of wine.

Falling in love with Philip Egerton? Madness. The

man had kept a mistress for years, had several by the sounds of it—the man had three daughters already!

Even now, she was not sure what had happened between him and Emma Tilbury.

Besides, she had been down this road before. With two broken engagements behind her, she was hardly eager to enter into a third, even with a far superior man.

"Oh—thank you," she said distractedly as a footman appeared behind her to take away her half-eaten dessert. "It…it was delicious."

Sophia could hardly remember what it tasted like, but with dessert done, the port and cheese would be brought through, and the ladies would retreat to the drawing room.

It would, admittedly, leave her alone with her mother, who was almost bursting with joy at the thought of having Philip as a son-in-law—but it would give her the chance to give her mother a good talking to, and cease that line once and for all.

"Dear me," said Mrs. Worsley, standing up and putting a hand to her face. "You know, I think I feel a little unwell. Arthur, can we call the carriage?"

Sophia opened her mouth, but Philip got there first.

"My dear Mrs. Worsley, you must permit me to assist you," he said quickly, rising to his feet. "My servants will ensure your carriage can be ready in a matter of minutes, and I beg you to allow me to give the order to take you home if that is what you wish?"

Mr. Worsley had risen now and taken his wife's arm in his own. "Mariah?"

"Oh, I just feel…" murmured Mrs. Worsley, her hand still on her forehead. "I am sure 'tis nothing, I assure you…"

"McCall, the Worsleys' carriage," snapped Philip, genuine concern on his face. "Mrs. Worsley is not well. Alert Doctor Sanders, and ask him to meet her at her rooms."

"'Tis such a shame, I so wished to stay for the entire evening," said Mrs. Worsley distractedly as the four of them rose to leave the dining room.

Sophia touched her mother's shoulder gently as they stood in the hallway. "You must not upset yourself, Mama."

"Nothing is more important than one's health," said Philip seriously. "The carriage will be here momentarily, Mrs. Worsley."

Sophia smiled, trying to show the gratitude she felt. It was unlike her mother to suddenly fall ill, all the more reason to get her home. Her parents may irritate her beyond the point of distraction, but they were her parents, and she loved them dearly.

"I will be right beside you in the carriage," Mr. Worsley was saying to his wife, her arm still tucked into his. "Ah, there is the door. The carriage is ready."

"Thank you," said Mrs. Worsley. "I do hope Sophia's company will be sufficient for you, your lordship, and I am again so sorry that we have to leave in such a rush."

Sophia removed her hand from her mother's shoulder and rolled her eyes. *She should have known—her mother was not unwell at all!* It was all a ruse, an attempt to ensure her daughter was alone with the earl.

"I am quite happy to accompany you in the carriage, Mother," Sophia said pointedly as her father helped her mother on with her pelisse. "Do you not think it is a little rebellious to leave me alone with..."

Her voice trailed away as she caught her mother's eye. It was clear Mrs. Worsley would make a real scene if she was not to be given her own way.

Really, sometimes Sophia was unsure which of them was the parent, which the rebel.

"Fine," she said heavily. "I will return home in Philip—in Marnmouth's carriage later—but not much later, mark me."

"You take all the time in the world, my dear, if you are enjoying yourself," said Mrs. Worsley faintly, and her husband helped her down the steps and into the carriage.

Sophia simply could not look at Philip. *By God, he must be able to see through this pathetic subterfuge easily!*

"And Doctor Sanders," he was saying to his butler seriously. "You must instruct him to meet the Worsleys—"

"All I need is rest, I am sure," came Mrs. Worsley's voice from the carriage. "Just rest. Have a lovely evening, you two."

The carriage rattled away, and Philip shut the door behind them.

Sophia swallowed. It was strange being alone with Philip in his house. Of course, she had been last night—but now her parents knew it. *What were they expecting?*

What was Philip expecting?

At this very moment, he was laughing. "Your mother should be on the stage. She is most excellent. So. What shall we do now?"

CHAPTER TWELVE

*B*Y GOD, *SHE was beautiful.* There Sophia stood, all innocence and laughter at her mother's ridiculous acting, and he knew that if he played his cards right, he would be given the chance to…

To do anything.

She was smiling coquettishly but did not speak. Philip swallowed. This was his first real opportunity to seduce her. True, she had been alone with him before, but the last time they had been together, she had wanted to ascertain whether he had come here to entangle himself once more in the arms of a mistress.

And those stolen kisses outside—well, they were nothing compared to what he wanted to do to her. *To slowly unpeel each layer of clothing off until the very essence of Sophia lay before him, ready for him to—*

"Tuppence."

Philip blinked. Sophia had spoken, but the

word did not make sense.

"Tuppence," she repeated with a smile. "For your thoughts."

He smiled wistfully and wondered just what she would do with the knowledge of those particular thoughts. *Run? Leap into his arms?*

"We should probably return to the drawing room," he said aloud. "Tuppence? Is the phrase not typically a penny?"

Sophia sat in an armchair, Philip cursing silently. He had not thought to indicate the sofa. *Now he had no chance to sit beside her, damn it!*

"Yes, usually," she said with a light smile. "But then, your thoughts looked so deep, and I thought they were at least worth tuppence."

It was impossible not to smile as he sat opposite her. *Sophia Worsley.* So witty, so pretty. Why on earth had those other churls left her at the altar? He could not make head nor tails of it, and the longer he spent in her company, the more ridiculous it got.

"Fine, a shilling," said Sophia, throwing up her hands in mock outrage. "But I will not be forced above that."

Philip smiled as he said without a second thought, "I was wondering why Beauvale did not marry you."

The teasing smile was wiped from Sophia's face, and the room fell into an awkward silence entirely of his own making.

What in God's name did he think he was doing? Of all the things to say—he could have said anything! After flattering and praising her mother so expertly all evening, too? He could woo Sophia, tease her, sweet-talk her, and what had he done?

Christ alive, but he did not deserve her if he was going to trot out nonsense like that.

"I mean," Philip said hastily, attempting to backtrack.

"No, calm yourself," said Sophia. Her voice was stiff, but the smile remained. "I am not surprised you have wondered. Many people do."

It looked as though she wished to continue, but she fell silent as her gaze drifted away and toward the fire.

"In many ways, it feels like a very long time ago," Sophia said unexpectedly in a soft voice. "'Tis hard to believe only a few months have passed. Of course, the first one was a little while ago now."

Philip swallowed. *The first one?*

"When I first met Robert, I was in my first Season at the rather early age of seventeen," said Sophia. "I think my mother was tired of attending balls, and my father abandoned her for the card tables. She wished to have a companion, and within a few weeks, I had met Robert."

Philip had never heard the name, but that was not too unexpected. People knew earls and dukes and such things. Earls did not know *people*.

"His parents did not approve, but mine did, and he was of age, and so the wedding plans began in earnest," said Sophia softly. "I did not love him. He was pleasant, and I was unsure whether I would meet with another gentleman I could stand."

"A common concern," said Philip gently.

She laughed. "Yes, I have met many a young lady with the same worry. Well, the story, at least, is short. Robert's father discovered our plans, threatened to cut him off without a penny, and he never turned up to the church on the wedding day."

Philip shook his head. Anger rose in his heart as though he had been there.

"Blaggard."

Sophia smiled wanly, her gaze darting to him and then returning to the blaze. "I'm uncertain now whether his actions were better or worse than Jacob. The latter was…enamored, shall we say, with another but did not consider that important information to share with me."

Philip thought but did not speak of the profound affection he had seen shared between the late Mrs. Howard, now Mrs. Beauvale, and her new husband. Yes, there was certainly something there that could not have been ignored—but to completely leave Sophia oblivious?

"And Jacob turned up on our wedding day,"

said Sophia with a roll of her eyes, "with his lady in the congregation. We managed to get as far as the vows, at which point I admit I believed we were safe, and just as he was about to declare himself for me…well, he stormed away, pulling her with him out of the church."

To his horror, Philip found his mouth was open, and he closed it hastily. It really was the most awful luck, and worse, she had had no control over the matters.

"Rascals and brigands," he managed to say. "They should be shot!"

Her laugh seemed more carefree than he had expected. "Yes, that is what I thought at the time. And yet…'tis strange. I was not much enamored with either of them. I…I cared because of my reputation. But my heart was not touched by either gentleman."

Her dancing eyes met his, pink rising in her cheeks. *What was she trying to tell him?* Was she suggesting, perhaps, that her heart was finally touched? She had, after all, stormed all the way to Bath after discovering he had left London. *What was that, if not passion!*

"I would hope, however," Philip added. *This had to be delicate.* "That neither of them…took advantage of you?"

"They absolutely took advantage of me!" Sophia retorted. "And my parents, too! I cannot believe it, sometimes. My poor parents paid for two weddings out of their own pockets, which never…"

Her voice trailed away as the true meaning of his words started to sink in.

"Oh," she said. "I see what you mean. No, they did not take advantage of me, despite our engagements. I still have that innocence to my name, at least."

Philip swallowed. It was a disrespectful question to ask, he knew, but his curiosity got the better of him. Besides, selfishly, he wanted to be the first man to show her what pleasure was.

"I would not worry about it if you had lost that innocence," he said as airily as he could muster. "In many situations, I would say 'tis better lost."

She really did laugh at that one, tucking one foot underneath her in the armchair. "How like a gentleman to think that way. Of course, it does not matter if *you* bed a few women. No one will think any the less of you—but woe betides any woman caught kissing a gentleman in the street! That is far too rebellious."

Her eyes sparkled despite the bitter tone of her voice, and Philip smiled. Sophia remembered those stolen kisses in London.

"Perhaps the rules are a little unfair, I admit," he said in a low voice. "But they are the rules we live by unless one decides to rebel against them. Like you do."

There was something utterly incomprehensible in her eyes as Sophia said, "Well, I have not rebelled that far. Not yet."

Was there an invitation in her voice? Philip worked to keep his breathing calm, but his heart beat frantically. She had created an opening in their conversation, and damnit, he was going to take it.

"You must have seen quite a few ladies lose their reputations, I mean," she continued. "Taken their innocence in many cases."

Philip laughed. "I am not that much older than you, really!"

"More than ten years," Sophia countered. "And I imagine you have had far more experience in…in these matters."

She was inquisitive, that much was obvious, but Philip hesitated before replying. There was naught wrong with curiosity. And he was older, wiser, and certainly more knowledgeable.

"True, I am older than you," he accepted, spreading out his hands. "But those additional years have brought a number of benefits—greater income and, as you point out, more experience with the ladies. I know what they want. I give them what they want."

Was that a shiver through Sophia's body? All he had to do was play his cards right, and he could be looking at a winning hand.

"I suppose age does have its advantages, yes,"

she said quietly, not quite meeting his gaze. "I have certainly noticed you are not...you are different from the gentlemen my age. Less foolish. More...more charming."

Rising and moving to the sofa where she had so wantonly kissed him before, Philip patted the empty seat beside him. "Why do you not join me, Miss Sophia Worsley?"

"Because you are trying to seduce me, Philip Egerton, Earl of Marnmouth."

"Yes, I am," he said rather seriously, "and it will be much easier if you come here."

Philip waited for Sophia's response. This was the true test, and not a decision he could force her to make quickly. If she decided to join him, then...then she was open to the idea of lovemaking.

If not...he would have to reconsider. Perhaps she would need something a little more firm in the way of an offer to consider allowing him access to that delectable body...

It was an eternity, but at last, Sophia rose elegantly from her seat, took the three steps across the room, and sat gently beside him.

Joy rose in Philip's stomach as he pushed down the impulse to kiss her immediately. *He would have her, but not yet.* Sophia deserved the absolute best. She should look back on this night and know it was not just her first, but the first of many.

Taking her hand in his, Philip smiled. "Seduction, what an ugly word. It sounds so conniving, so cold when all I feel about you…is warmth."

Not taking his eyes from hers, he gently started to caress her hand, allowing his fingers to stray toward her wrist but never further.

"You are very bold," she said.

Philip nodded. "If one wishes to win the heart of a lady, one has to be bold. You have made me bold, Sophia, ever since I met you. Ever since I saw you in Almack's, I have known what I wanted. I think I offered it to you right then."

His fingers continued to lightly stroke her arm, and he felt her quiver.

"You were daring then, and you are daring now," said Sophia hesitantly. "Losing one's innocence is no quick decision. What makes you think you are worthy?"

He paused. *It was a good question.* "Because I will, at the very least, commit to our lovemaking and follow through. Nothing more, nothing less."

Sophia chuckled. "And this is the great seduction?"

Philip smiled. *She was ready for him.*

"No," he said, looking deep into her eyes and vowing he would never let anything harm her. "No, the seduction is when I do not just kiss you, but kiss you so joyously that you tremble in my arms. When I kiss you so tenderly, you cry out, desperate for more."

His fingers started to tease their way up her arm, always moving, always stroking.

"And I will give you more. I will slowly tease and touch every part of you," whispered Philip. "Then, just when you think you cannot stand it any longer, I will remove your clothing as you cry my name."

His voice was so soft, Sophia leaned forward to hear him—that, or she wanted to kiss him immediately. Philip leaned back. *Desire always started in anticipation.* Focusing his gaze on her mouth, he felt her pulse quicken. She wanted him. She was ready, but he would still warm her up with his words. *This had to be perfect.*

"And then I will teach you," he murmured. "Teach you just what pleasure is. Just when you think you cannot bear any more, I will show you ecstasy we can share, and we will."

There was a gasp so slight, Philip thought he had imagined it. Sophia was looking as though she wished to melt into his arms and vow to be his for the rest of her life.

"*That* is a seduction, Sophia. The most rebellious thing a lady can do. Are you ready?"

Just as the evening before, Sophia could not contain herself. She leaned forward and kissed him, and at that moment, Philip tasted sweet relief.

Now with Sophia in his arms and his lips on hers, Philip knew what he was going to do, and he shivered at the expected pleasure they would both enjoy. *This would be a night neither of them would forget.*

His tongue teased her lips, her mouth so sweet and tender, as Philip gently moved her so they were lying on the sofa together.

"Oh, Sophia," he murmured, unable to help himself. "God, you are so beautiful."

His hands had quickly moved to her breasts, and he almost moaned aloud to finally have his hands on that which had sorely tempted him so often. *Christ, she was so sweet.*

"Philip," she cried as he started to kiss down her neck. "Mmm…"

Sophia clung to him, arms around his neck.

At first, his hand gently stroked her thigh through her gown. As she writhed underneath him and allowed her legs to part, Philip's fingers quickly moved the heavy skirts of her gown, and they both gasped as his fingers came into contact with her thigh.

"Oh, Philip, no one has—no one has ever," Sophia began, but Philip stopped her mouth with a kiss.

She did not have to explain to him. He already knew, could already tell in the way she trembled at his touch.

Philip continued kissing her fiercely as his hand moved slowly but inexorably toward that secret place which he had been so desperate to stroke.

"What?" Sophia's eyes widened in shock as his fingers first brushed past her secret place, but then, "Oh, yes!"

The moan was enough to make his manhood jerk, but Philip attempted to ignore it. *This was not about him, not yet. This was about her. Sophia.* She deserved so much, so the least he could do was worship her.

Just as his fingers started to pick up their pace, Philip gritted his teeth and stopped.

Sophia's eyes flew open. "More, Philip, please."

It took all his self-control to say, "No, sweet. Not yet. We need to get these clothes off you first."

"What—what, here?"

Philip smiled. "Of course here."

Sophia laughed. "But—but…you are mad!"

Philip stepped away. It was torture to leave her, but necessary. The key was still in the drawing room door, and as he turned it, he heard the satisfying click of the lock.

"I do this sometimes if…" Philip swallowed.

"Do not concern yourself. This is hardly a proposal," she said. "I am hardly ignorant of your other women."

Philip nodded and strode across the room. *There were usually—yes, here they were.* In one swift movement, he pulled out the bundle of furs that he had left here for just such an occasion and laid them before the fire.

"Come here," he growled.

Sophia obeyed him immediately, lust and desire in her eyes. He captured her lips with his own as his fingers started to make light work of her gown, fumbling only slightly.

Her hands were not idle. They reached for his coat, his waistcoat, and his shirt until all were undone, and it was but a moment for her to push them aside and reveal his chest.

Philip smiled as he pulled down her gown, leaving her in her undershift.

"Are you—"

"Certain?" Sophia gasped, pulling at her undershift to remove it. "Absolutely."

It fell to the floor in a pool of linen, and Philip had to swallow to keep his concentration. *By God, she was perfect.* Every inch designed to tempt a gentleman to betray himself, to do anything she wanted.

"Now you," she whispered.

Pulling off his breeches in such haste he was sure a button flew off, he grinned as he grabbed her and lifted Sophia off her feet until they were entwined on the rugs as nature had intended them.

It was enough to push any man over the edge.

Kissing passionately led him to tease her thighs, stroking carefully as his fingers moved closer and closer to her secret place, and she moaned. "Please, Philip."

How could he ignore such a request? His fingers found their home once again in her wetness, and it was not difficult after heating her up so wildly, to bring her closer and closer until her breathing was ragged.

"That's enough of that," he said teasingly, removing his fingers just as he felt the vibrations of her pleasure start to build.

The cry of disappointment Sophia made was enough to make him weep.

"You—you!" Sophia's eyes came into focus as she grabbed his hand and moved it back into position. "You finish what you started!"

Philip groaned. His fingers resumed their frantic rhythm, and Sophia cried out in shock as she came around him. It was a full minute before she was able to focus her gaze on him, but it was accompanied by a smile.

"You were right," she breathed. "I had no idea about pleasure. What is that?"

"It prevents a child," he said, breath ragged, pulling on a protective. "Now come here."

He entered her slowly, expecting at any moment Sophia would cry out in pain. But she did not. His preparation of her, his devotion to her pleasure first, had done its work.

"Oh, Philip, yes," she murmured, wriggling underneath him on the furs in a most distracting way. "And...and there is more?"

"So much more," he moaned as he kissed her, manhood desperate for movement.

It did not take long to bring Sophia to ecstasy once more. She was eager for him and now knew the path to pleasure. It almost overwhelmed him, seeing her lose control, and it was with great care that Philip slowed his rhythm and then built it up to bring her to pleasure for a third time before finally letting himself go.

It was only afterward that he realized he had collapsed beside her. *Christ alive, but he had done it. He had seduced Sophia Worsley—or, perhaps, she had seduced him. He was not sure.*

"Is that all, then?" Sophia said with a sleepy smile.

Philip pulled her into his arms. "Not even close, but you will have to forgive me. That will have to be another day."

She laughed. "You would be fortunate indeed if you think you're getting that again."

"I would be," he whispered, unable to put his emotions into words. "I will be."

"You are very sure of yourself."

Philip nuzzled against her, kissing Sophia's forehead. "I am very sure of you."

What nonsense, what pleasant nothings they whispered to each other, and as Sophia started to fall asleep and her breathing slowed, Philip knew he had made the right decision.

Mistress, wife, he did not care. As long as Sophia was in his life, he would be complete.

CHAPTER THIRTEEN

S OPHIA LEANED AGAINST the front door, reliant on its strength to keep her upright.

The rooms the Worsleys had taken in Bath were silent.

Wild thoughts scattered through Sophia's mind, none making sense, save one.

Philip. Philip Egerton, the man who had rushed into her life and entirely turned it upside down.

The gentleman she had allowed to do…

She smiled. *Well, everything.* His seduction was now complete. She had given him everything, all of herself, holding nothing back.

It had not been difficult, keeping her innocence during her previous two engagements.

Now she had lost that innocence, willingly so, to a man who had made her no promises. No words of love had crept through his lips, no protestations of affection, and best of all, no ridiculous pronouncements of marriage.

This was what she had wanted. An encounter on her terms. She had not allowed any hopes for nonsense promises that would immediately be broken. A true rebel. The breeches were a signal to the world that she was no longer going to accept its rules and regulations on her, but that had been easy.

Breeches? Easily put on and easily removed.

This was different. She had permitted a gentleman to take from her something she could never get back, and yet no regret seared her heart.

Even in her wildest dreams, her imagination could not have predicted such pleasure. That a gentleman and lady could enjoy each other in such a way—that the closeness afforded them by chance or stolen opportunity could lead to such things!

Sophia's smile faded. She certainly would not have predicted that such an innocent dinner, and one with her parents to boot, could have ended in such a scandalous way.

Sophia swallowed. It was scandalous, she knew, *wanton* to think such thoughts. Ladies were not supposed to enjoy lovemaking. No, it was for the creation of children and nothing else—it was gentlemen who could enjoy such things.

Except—except she had enjoyed it. What had that man done to her?

She would not become Philip's mistress. Other ladies had, and they undoubtedly gained pleasure in his arms—but it had not lasted. Even Emma Tilbury, who had secured his affections for years, was now estranged—that's what the tittle-tattle of society said.

She certainly did not wish to become Philip's wife. She had suffered through enough engagements to last a lifetime.

But to experience that pleasure every night…

If only they could keep it a secret from her parents, from the world. If there were no lasting consequences, no children, if they were careful. *Why should she not take what she wanted?*

"Ah, there you are."

Sophia jumped.

Her father had walked into the hallway with a slightly distracted air holding the morning's paper. "Early morning walk?"

Sophia nodded, not trusting her voice. *Thank God she had thought to pull her pelisse closely around herself.* Mr. Worsley had not noticed his daughter was wearing the same gown and bonnet at their dinner with the Earl of Marnmouth the evening before.

"Y-Yes," she nodded rather breathlessly. "Yes, Father. If you will excuse me, the wind is very… I will go upstairs and adjust my hair before breakfast."

Mr. Worsley nodded and smiled. "You know,

I did not have the chance to say yesterday, your mother performing so…I wished you to know both I and your mother like the earl very much. Well done…"

Voice trailing away as his gaze moved from his daughter to his newspaper, her father wandered into the breakfast room.

Sophia breathed out slowly. *She had been fortunate.* If she had met her mother in the hallway, Mrs. Worsley's beady eyes would undoubtedly have realized there was something amiss—and what a to-do that would have been.

Racing up the stairs two at a time, her looking glass showed a woman with flushed cheeks, bright eyes, and hair utterly tangled underneath her bonnet. *Her father really was unobservant,* Sophia decided as she dragged a hairbrush through her tangled mane.

Yet, he was not entirely to blame. As Sophia examined her reflection, she was surprised to see that she was unaltered in many ways from the day before.

"Sophia!"

She straightened abruptly, head spinning at the sound of her mother's voice.

"Sophia, breakfast!"

Hastily grabbing hairpins, Sophia attempted to make herself look respectable. Quickly pulling on another gown, she stepped into the breakfast room, still tying up the bodice.

"Ah, good morning, Sophia," said her mother, showing no signs of ill health.

"Good morning," she said with a wink at her father. "I am pleased to see you so well recovered, Mother. I was concerned last night you may have been taken seriously unwell."

Mrs. Worsley shot her daughter a look but evidently could find no hint of sarcasm in her tones. "Yes, I was fortunate to recover so quickly."

"And to what does Doctor Sanders ascribe your miraculous recovery?"

This time Sophia knew she had gone too far.

"Doctor Sanders was sent packing, as you well know!" Her mother spoke firmly as she buttered a piece of toast. "'Twas all for you, Sophia, and I will accept your thanks now."

Sophia poured herself some tea. "I know not to what you are referring, Mother, and I hope you would never feign a serious injury for my benefit. I had a pleasant evening, returned home, and now here we are."

Well, she thought to herself, *it was not entirely a falsehood.* She had experienced a very pleasant evening, and she had returned home. *That morning.*

"It was lovely indeed to meet your friend, the Earl of Marnmouth," said Mrs. Worsley delicately.

Sophia glanced at her father, still buried in his

newspaper. *So, the interrogation was about to begin.* At least she had expected it, and there was no chance she would reveal how she felt truly about Philip.

"The Earl of Marnmouth," she said decidedly, choosing a piece of toast, "is not my friend."

Mrs. Worsley glanced at her husband and must have nudged him under the table, for he suddenly placed his newspaper down, scowled at his wife, and then peered at his daughter.

"Not a friend, eh?" he said gruffly. "What is he then?"

Sophia opened her mouth, closed it again, and began to furiously lather marmalade over her slice of toast.

What was Philip? It was a question she had not seriously considered. She had no wish to give her parents false hope, so surely the less she said, the better. An indifferent acquaintance was the best way to proceed.

Taking a sip of tea, Sophia tried to marshal her thoughts. *How to describe a man with whom she had just made love as an indifferent acquaintance?*

"Well, whatever he is, I hope the earl remains in our acquaintance. I would like to be more intimately acquainted with him," said Mrs. Worsley grandly. "Such a gentleman."

Mr. Worsley nodded. "His knowledge of shooting is first rate, I must say. I hope one day to visit him at Marnmouth Heights, the grouse shooting he described—"

"And the décor of his home, truly spectacular. I have not seen anything like it since visiting the Duke of Devonshire," said Mrs. Worsley. "Wealth and taste do not always go hand in hand, of course, it is so pleasing to see a gentleman take an interest…"

Sophia allowed them to talk, seeing with relief, they had enough opinions on Philip to entertain themselves—at least, for now.

Besides, what could she contribute? She had no interest in shooting or wallpaper in the slightest.

No, she was more intrigued by his character. The fact he had three daughters would probably not be of interest to her parents—*or rather, would not endear him to them.*

Why did she want to endear Philip to them? Was that not what she had fought against since they had first made his acquaintance? It would be foolish to the extreme to allow her parents to realize just how much more she knew of the earl. Far more than she should. More than was acceptable for a young lady.

"—for you, though I had not thought any of our circle was aware we were in Bath already. I *said*, Sophia, this is for you."

Sophia jumped, startled from her reverie.

"Someone is thinking of their beloved," said Mrs. Worsley with a knowing look.

Sophia rolled her eyes. "I beg your pardon,

Father?"

She had not been paying attention for a good while, for the post had been brought in. Three letters sat on a silver tray in the middle of the breakfast table, and one of them had her name on the front.

Miss Sophia Worsley

"I do not recognize the handwriting, but that is no great matter. I have no eye for such a thing," mused her father, holding the letter up to his eyes.

Sophia held out her hand. "Thank you, Father."

As he passed it over, it turned toward her mother, who exclaimed, "Is that—there is a seal on the back, Arthur!"

Thankfully, Mr. Worsley had released the missive into Sophia's hand. Her mother was correct. There was a seal marked in the wax on the back. It was a large and rather ornate W.

"A double-u," she said aloud.

Her mother visibly sagged. "Oh. Do we know any families with the name of double-u?"

"There is always Beauvale," said Mr. Worsley looking a little discomforted. "His middle name is William, though I do not know why he would use his middle name…"

Sophia swallowed. There was certainly no

reason why Jacob would be writing to her—he had broken their engagement, he had paid her parents most of the money expended on the preparations, and that had been an end to it.

Or so she thought.

Carefully lifting the seal from the page to keep it intact, Sophia unfolded the letter and read the short note inside.

Sophia,

I would be grateful if you would meet me on the corner of Milsom Street and George Street, where you and I could take a short walk. I will, of course, return you home before dark.

Shall we say eleven o'clock?

I remain your faithful servant,
Philip Egerton, Marnmouth

Sophia almost laughed aloud. *Of course. Not a W, but an M. She had been holding the letter upside down.*

She glanced up at her parents. Sighing, she knew what she had to do but it would only exchange concern for false hopes.

"'Tis from the Earl of Marnmouth," she said heavily.

Immediately, her parents' expressions altered. Her father's furrowed brow disappeared, and her mother's worry was transformed into excitement. "Oh, my dear Sophia, an offer!"

"Not an offer," said Sophia hastily. *The last thing she needed was their imaginations.* "An offer to meet for a walk. Today. In an hour, in fact."

"Well, that is very gracious of him, I am sure, but I believe someone should go with you," said Mr. Worsley heavily. "A young lady, unchaperoned. 'Tis not to be borne."

"No—no, I would rather see him alone."

As soon as the words were out of her mouth, Sophia realized her mistake. Her parents exchanged an excited look.

"Mother, Father, I do not know where you have this idea from, but Philip—Marnmouth," she corrected hastily. *Damn!* "The earl does not wish to marry me."

Mr. Worsley winked. "Of course not, my dear. Your secret is safe with me."

Sophia sighed. *No point continuing this conversation.* "Please, may I be excused?"

"You may," said Mrs. Worsley with excitement. "And give our love to Marnmouth, any that you can spare!"

It was with bad grace, therefore, that Sophia strode out of their rooms half an hour later, on her way to Milsom Street. If only Philip had found a way to get the letter to her without her parents knowing. *They really were incorrigible.*

Although a few minutes early, Philip was already there. He smiled broadly as she approached, bowing low as she curtseyed.

"I did not think you would be here," Sophia said as a greeting. *Well, what was the proper address for a gentleman with whom you had last been naked?*

"I sent the letter from here," admitted Philip. "'Tis amazing what one can do with a little silver."

He stepped forward to embrace her, but Sophia stepped back into the path of another.

"Not here," she said quietly, cheeks pink. "Not in public."

Philip nodded. "Shall we walk then?"

Sophia nodded. *What did he want? What could he wish to say, to share that could not be done in the privacy of his rooms?*

Her heart may be confused and unsure, but she knew one thing. She would not commit to anybody, not anymore. Seeing Philip in the light of day had brought her that certainty. She had made love to him, and that was it. She could not do that again, not if he wanted to exact promises from her. She could not risk her heart becoming too entangled.

As they walked through Milsom Street, Philip said in a low voice, "I am so happy, you know."

Sophia nodded. "I...I still cannot believe I—that we..."

Words failed her.

"You really are the rebel now, aren't you?" Philip teased.

She took a deep breath as they turned a corner. "Yes, but…but not again. I cannot do it again."

There was a little regret tinging her words, but Sophia knew it was the right thing to do. *She would not be his wife, and being his mistress would only lead to him putting her aside one day, and she could not…she would not be able to bear it.*

The image of Emma Tilbury forced its way into her mind. She had enjoyed Philip's attentions and then lost them. Lost him.

Sophia glanced at Philip's face and saw true disappointment.

"Look, I care for you, Sophia," he said slowly, keeping his voice low so no one else could hear. "But more than that, I respect you. I will never… I would never do anything to make you uncomfortable. You are the one in charge here."

Sophia smiled. His respect for her was intoxicating, so unlike any of the yobbish gentlemen she had endured over her years in society.

Leaning forward to impetuously kiss him on the cheek, she said, "I am not saying you will never be able to persuade me, but—well, I am not your mistress, Philip, and certainly not your wife. We will continue on my terms or not at all."

Philip raised his hand to touch his cheek where she had kissed him. "Sophia—"

"And do not read anything else into that kiss!" she said hastily with a grin. "Look, I must go back home, or my parents will think we are engaged!"

With a laugh, Sophia turned away and forced herself not to look back.

CHAPTER FOURTEEN

"AH, THERE HE is! I thought you had got lost, Braedon, but Bath simply isn't that big!"

Philip grinned as McCall showed in the last of the party to arrive—Abraham Fitzclarence, Viscount Braedon, who looked sodden.

"'Tis a downpour out there!" said Braedon. "I don't know how you two managed to avoid it!"

The Earl of Chester and the Duke of Larnwick grinned at the bedraggled Braedon, hair slicked to his head, coat dripping onto the floor, and boots making horrible little squelching sounds on the carpet.

"Goodness, yes, you are a little damp," said Philip with a laugh. "McCall, would you mind taking the viscount upstairs and helping him to dry off? There should be enough things of mine he can borrow for the evening."

"Of course, your lordship," bowed the butler.

"This way, sir."

Braedon made a pretty pathetic figure as he trooped out.

Chester laughed with a shake of his head. "Poor old Braedon! He always manages to draw the short straw!"

Philip nodded as Larnwick continued to chuckle. He had ridden back to London for a few days, officially in an attempt to clear his head, and had invited his friends over for some sort of distraction. Larnwick and Chester were always good company, and Braedon…*well, he was always certain to bring laughter into the room, whether he intended to or not.*

After ten minutes, Braedon made another appearance in his drawing room, this time looking a little less damp and a lot more cheerful.

"Thank you, awfully, Marnmouth," he said with a smile. "If I am honest, I was surprised at the invitation at all, and I am most grateful for the lending of your clothes."

"Surprised at my invitation?" Philip inquired, indicating Braedon should be seated by the fire. "Why?"

It was with a sheepish look that Braedon sagged into the armchair. "Well, I always manage to put my foot in it somehow!"

"Yes, you certainly do!" grinned Chester, handing the newcomer a glass and bottle of red wine. "But as 'tis usually a complete accident, we tend to let you off!"

Philip laughed. *Yes, this was what he needed. A distraction.* A chance to let off steam without any thoughts of Sophia—*damn. Any more thoughts of Sophia, certainly.*

"I would offer you a drink, Braedon, but as Chester has done such a capital job already, I will say this is a casual evening, and I do not expect many opportunities for you to embarrass yourself," said Philip. "I have gone to no trouble."

"No trouble?" Larnwick said with an appreciative smack of his lips as he drained his glass. "A little trouble, but not much, precisely how I like an evening. Good wine, good cards, good company, 'tis all I need."

"Besides, you have brought a few bottles yourself," added Philip with an appreciative nod. "And now Braedon is here. I fear we may need them!"

Raucous laughter echoed around the candle-lit drawing room as the gentlemen lounged by the fireplace, carelessly taking potshots at each other.

Philip smiled. *Yes, this had been a good idea—a chance for him to spend a little more time in male company, rather than female.* Sophia may have caused disappointment by her refusal to commit to any more dalliances, but she had been right about one thing.

It was too easy to become… infatuated was a

strong word. His gaze drifted to the fur still lying before the fireplace and tried to forget that only a few days ago, he had been making love to Sophia.

"You—you! You finish what you started!"

The damned fire kept drawing his eye, and each time it simply reminded him of Sophia. *Her lips, her mouth, the way she had cried out...*

"And how go the wedding plans?"

Larnwick sighed heavily and helped himself to another glass of wine. "Miss Madam is still undecided about so many things that the wedding has been put back again—ye would nae credit it, would ye!"

All his companions laughed as he slipped into Scots, brow furrowed in irritation.

"You know, it seems you have been engaged for years," Philip mused.

Chester crowed, "He has!"

Larnwick shook his head with a wry smile as he passed the bottle to Braedon. "Two and a half years and counting. Who knows how long before I finally bring the woman to bed!"

Braedon snorted. "You haven't already?"

"You think the Lymingtons would permit me anywhere near her if I had? You think the wedding would not have occurred?" shot back the Scotsman. "Nae, 'tis rare indeed to have an engagement this long, but I am not so concerned. 'Tis hardly a love match, and the longer it goes on, the older and wiser my bride should be."

Philip stepped to the cabinet where he kept his cigars so he could hide his red cheeks from his friends. He had done far more with Sophia than Larnwick had enjoyed with his own betrothed, but *he* had not proposed...

"Cigars," he said, handing them around.

Chester took one before saying, "If you ask me, it sounds like you do not care for her."

Shrugging, Larnwick accepted a cigar. "Not many of us have your luck, Chester—you like your bride, and you liked her before you wed her!"

"Yes, indeed," said Braedon, evidently eager to join in the conversation as Philip sat down. "'Tis rare indeed, although I do hope for it."

His wistful tone was unlike Braedon, and Philip cast him a glance surreptitiously under the guise of handing him his tinderbox.

Was there something deeper about Braedon he had never noticed before? The man was a bumbling bag of awkwardness, a strange one—and what had that strange conversation at the Larnwick Ball been about? He had utterly forgotten about it until this moment.

"Not all of us can have mistresses!" Larnwick was saying, and laughter once again rang out around the room—this time, Philip knew, at his own expense.

"Ah, you can all laugh, but I have not had Miss Tilbury with me, nor any other mistress for some time now."

Braedon nodded as he blew out billows of smoke. "Yes, two years and four months."

The drawing room fell silent. He coughed, smoke blossoming everywhere.

"My word," said Philip dryly. "Have you been counting how long it has been since I bedded Emma Tilbury?"

He had intended it as a jest. It was a ridiculous idea, and no one would do such a thing.

"No, no, I just…well, I have a memory for these things."

Philip nodded. He was not a cruel man and wouldn't embarrass Braedon purposefully, but it was a strange thing to say. Braedon had no great memory. *What was he hiding?*

In an attempt to move the conversation away from Braedon, he said nonchalantly, "In truth, I have seen far more of Miss Sophia Worsley than Miss Emma Tilbury recently."

Chester and Braedon laughed, exchanging knowing looks, whereas Larnwick just looked blank. "Miss who?"

"Oh, come now, Larnwick, you must have seen her!" Braedon crowed, evidently relieved the focus had shifted. "The lady who turns up to balls and parties in breeches?"

Now it was Philip's turn to feel uncomfortable. Most unfair of Braedon it was, seated there in Philip's chair, in Philip's clothes, only enjoying a laugh because Philip had not teased him.

"Not to everything," he said awkwardly. "I believe she wore a gown to your ball, Larnwick, which is why you may not have noticed her."

"And yet she has become notorious for wearing them," said Chester, leaning back and breathing in the heady cigar smoke.

Larnwick's eyes were wide. "My God, what a rebel!"

"Ah, and that is where you are wrong," said Braedon with all the confidence of an expert. "Miss Worsley thinks she is a rebel, true, but she is wrong."

Philip shifted in his seat. *He had not really thought about it, but of course, Sophia was closer to Braedon and Chester's ages than his own.* They undoubtedly knew her, had known her for far longer than he had.

"You see, Miss Worsley has the protection of her parents, a steady income thanks to them, and when they sadly depart this earth, she will be very rich indeed," said Braedon knowledgeably. "The rebellious gals are those who leave it all behind or never had that security to begin with."

"I have heard her called a rebel," Chester mused. "but I admit I cannot think what she is rebelling against."

Philip's mouth was dry. *He had to speak, but what could he say without betraying her confidence?*

"Ah, one of those," said Larnwick with a nod.

"Yes, I know what you mean. Many of the bluestockings I have met are the same—happy to rebel in their way, but only until they go home at night to a warm house and a full stomach."

Now heat was searing Philip's chest. It had been thoughtless to bring her up at a gentlemanly evening, and the last thing he wanted was Sophia to be laughed at.

"I would say she is a rebel then," he said, attempting to broaden the conversation. "A lady, a gentleman's daughter? I would then say that breeches and so forth are more rebellious. No one would care if she were simply a maid."

All eyes focused on him, curiosity in every face.

"You…you have known Miss Worsley long?" asked Larnwick.

Chester leaned forward. "I did not know that, Marnmouth. Perhaps we have other acquaintances in common. Do you know—"

"No, no, not long," said Philip, hating himself for even bringing her up. "Just these last few weeks."

A long whistle came from the mouth of Braedon as he tapped his cigar ash into the ashtray. "So…since her last broken engagement, then?"

"Last one?" said Larnwick quickly.

Damn. Damn and blast his stupid mouth for mentioning her in the first place. Philip knew it would be difficult to entirely direct them onto a different conversational path, but hopefully, if he was clever…

"These cigars, by the way, are not to be spoken of outside this room," he said with a false jovial air. "I had to procure them from a very—"

"Come on now, a smattering of gossip will do me good!" Larnwick interrupted.

Chester grinned. "'Tis hardly gossip, everyone in society knows. Besides, from what I have seen, Miss Worsley makes no secret of it."

Philip was forced to swallow down his ire as Chester started to explain the whole sordid affair to Larnwick, Braedon jumping in now and again to add details.

Christ alive, but he was a fool. That was his trouble. Sophia was always uppermost in his thoughts, so when he had picked a new conversational topic out of the air, she was the first thing he thought of!

Sophia would hate the thought of gentlemen discussing her. Philip had to hide his true feelings for her if they continued to talk of her much longer. He was not her father nor brother to defend her, and he did not want to open himself to some very uncomfortable questions…

Larnwick whistled slowly. "Two broken engagements? 'Tis very bad luck."

Philip saw his opening. "Yes, bad luck. Speaking of luck, shall I get the cards out?"

Sadly, none of his guests seemed interested in cards.

"Gossip? I would not call that the gossip about Miss Worsley," said Braedon eagerly.

Philip saw in horror that the half-empty bottle of wine which had been passed to the viscount not five minutes ago was now empty.

"The real gossip is why the second betrothal went on so long when it was so obvious Beauvale had lost interest," continued Braedon with a grin.

Larnwick leaned forward. "What do you mean, Braedon?"

"Now *that* is gossip," said Chester firmly. "I would hope we are above that, gentlemen."

But for the first time since her name had been mentioned by him, Philip now wished to hear more. *The real reason?*

He could not be seen to be encouraging it, not sharing that sort of illicit gossip in his own home. But Sophia had entranced him for too long. He could see there was more going on behind her eyes than she shared.

Something had happened in that engagement. Something she had not told him.

Braedon was looking pleased with himself. "Well, I think we all know that Jacob Beauvale is now married. The Honorable Mrs. Howard, as was, which is all well and good—but then, there is the child."

"Child?" *Good grief, it surely couldn't be—*

Sophia didn't have a child, had she?

Braedon grinned. *Why wouldn't the damn man speak?*

"Yes, Mrs. Howard had a child," said Braedon slowly. "She was with child when her first husband died, but the gossip was, and I see no reason to disbelieve it…well. That the father was Jacob himself."

Braedon leaned back with an impressive air on his face as Chester shook his head.

Philip tried not to let his sigh of relief be too apparent as his heart slowed. The Beauvale child, of course. He had forgotten.

"That is truly shocking," said Larnwick slowly.

"And Sophia—Miss Worsley knew this?" Philip found himself asking, unable to help himself.

Braedon looked triumphant. "Not only did Miss Worsley know about it, but I heard she attempted to blackmail Jacob to go through with the marriage."

Silence followed his words.

"No," said Chester with an air of finality. "No, *that* I cannot believe. Sophia Worsley?"

"I heard it from a very reputable source," said Braedon. "He, Beauvale, realized he had fallen in love with the Howard woman and attempted to do the right thing, but Miss Worsley was having none of it. She tried to force the marriage to completion, pushing the poor man to a breaking point at the wedding."

"So she clung onto him, and in that clinging, pushed him even further away?" said Larnwick slowly.

Braedon nodded. "That is what lost him. It was all her fault."

"Now, that is uncalled for," Chester said hastily. "Really! None of us know the poor girl enough, 'tis only gossip that Braedon has picked up from—"

"Someone intimately acquainted with all parties," Braedon interrupted. "Besides, it makes the most sense."

Larnwick was shaking his head. "Poor bairn though, to be jilted in such a fashion. Could her father not do anything?"

The conversation continued. Philip's mind was swimming with the information he had just heard, unable to untangle the rush of emotions it sparked in his soul.

Sophia Worsley. Blackmailer? It did not fit the woman he knew, but then, he had only known her for…what, a few months at most? Who knew what a lady would do to ensure a husband. Why had she not told him of all this before?

Philip tried desperately to think back and remember the conversations he had enjoyed with Sophia.

Swallowing down his bitterness, Philip took a deep breath and picked up his cigar. Sophia had made him no promises, just as he had made her no promises. It was clear, however, that they had much to talk about. *When could he see her? Why did his very skin crave her touch?*

"I thought you would have known all this, Marnmouth."

Philip blinked and saw Braedon looking at him closely. "What?"

"Why, I would have thought Miss Worsley would have mentioned this to you in your conversations," said Braedon with a knowing smile. "But I suppose 'tis only right the lady should have some secrets. After all, I am sure she does not know about all your mistresses!"

There were chuckles from Chester, and Philip smiled wanly. "No, just the one."

Emma. What would she have made of all this? It was the first time since they had parted that her opinion would truly have aided him; her ability to balance his raging emotions desperately needed.

"Right then," Philip said bracingly, pulling out a deck of cards. "A full hand each, gentle-men?"

They had an appetite for cards now, but Philip lost almost every hand, unable to concentrate. *Sophia.* She was the reason his mind slipped away from the game.

She had led a difficult life. True, she was a

lady, a gentleman's daughter, but she had been let down by love. Blackmailer or not, she had been desperate, unable to bear another broken engagement—which, irony of ironies, she was then forced to endure.

Sophia had taken on the burden of being society's jokes, but no longer. Philip was decided. He would put right those wrongs. He would give Sophia her dignity back.

He would marry her.

CHAPTER FIFTEEN

S OPHIA REMOVED HER bonnet happily, pulling a few autumnal leaves from where the wind had lodged them.

Autumn was her favorite season. The whistling of the wind, the bright sunshine that didn't overheat, the long walks of which she was so fond. The Worsleys had never been in Bath this early before, and the sweeping avenues, beautiful in their full color, were enough to soar joy in her heart as nothing else could.

Well. Other than Philip.

Only as she dropped the last golden leaf onto the floor did Sophia realize the house was not, as she had expected, empty. Her parents had spoken of going for a carriage ride to the countryside that afternoon, and yet noises of conversation emanated from the drawing room.

And not just her parents. There were the high sweet tones of her mother and the deep tones of her father. She would know them anywhere. But amongst them was a third voice. Someone she knew but could not immediately pick out from her memory.

The voice was low, controlled, and yet strange. It was hardly able to get a word in edgeways—which considering her mother, was perhaps not surprising.

Stepping closer to the drawing room, Sophia tilted head and caught a murmur that was a little louder. Her heart started to frantically flutter.

It was Philip!

No—was it? She leaned against the wall, trying to keep her breathing steady as she listened. Yes, she was almost willing to swear it was Philip inside that room. *With her parents.*

Sophia tried to think. *What on earth was Philip doing here?* They had made no appointment to meet—it had only been days ago since they had met on the corner of Milsom Street, and she had barely started to unravel her feelings about him since.

Even if he had arrived unannounced, there was no need for him to stay once he realized he had missed her. Although it was entirely possible that her parents would invite him in…

Yes, perhaps that was it. Sophia swallowed, trying to force down her panic. There was no possibility Philip would reveal their…assignation to her parents. *That would be madness.*

Still, the very thought of them talking about goodness knows what was enough to tense her shoulders. Despite knowing it was wrong, Sophia leaned an ear toward the door in the hope of catching a little of their conversation.

If it was about her, she reasoned, *then it was not precisely eavesdropping. Not really.*

Besides, she would be entering the room in a few minutes. She was only ascertaining the topic of conversation so she could join in.

Heart still fluttering, she closed her eyes to better concentrate.

"—admit myself pleased," her father's voice said, muffled through the wood of the door. "As is her mother."

There was a squeal which could only be Mrs. Worsley. "Oh, yes, very pleased!"

Sophia frowned. *Pleased?* Her parents were easily pleased, but it was most unlike them to share their joy with a relative stranger. Unless Philip had brought some books for them? Perhaps his bookseller had known they had a few on order which they had been unable to collect, so hasty was their departure from London.

She bit her lip. *That did not make much sense. Pleased? What for?*

"'Tis all rather quick, I know," came the low murmur of Philip's voice.

Sophia's heart skipped a beat. Just hearing him speak was enough to make her long for his touch. *It was ridiculous, this power he had over her. What was quick?* Had the books arrived far swifter than the bookseller had proposed? *What was going on?*

"That is how it is, sometimes," her father said hastily.

There was movement in the room; someone was walking around as though unable to sit still. Though every instinct urged her to step inside, Sophia held back.

What were they pleased about? Was it a walk, perhaps? Another dinner? It would certainly be swift, to organize another dinner as they had dined together so recently.

Perhaps that was it. *Her parents certainly liked Philip,* Sophia thought wryly, *though they approved of him as a future son-in-law, not simply as a gentleman.*

"And you think Sophia will be pleased?"

That was Philip's voice, and there was nervousness Sophia had never heard before.

Philip, uncertain? It was not the Marnmouth she knew. Maybe he—

"Of course, our daughter will be prodigiously pleased," her mother said.

Sophia grinned. Even through the door, she could hear the uncertainty in her mother's words. So, it was a plan that involved her—this dinner, or walk, or whatever it was—and they were unsure whether she would approve of it.

That sounded likely. She had hated the enforced dinners with Jacob, and whenever she had wished to dine at the Devonshires, despite their great and impressive title, her father had always inquired how many single gentlemen of good fortune would also be attending.

"We will have to ensure she finds out slowly, or she may buck at the proposal," said her father. "There is no one like Sophia for getting in the way of her own happiness."

Sophia thought that a little rich. After all, all she had done was what she had been told her whole life, and it was not as though she had attracted misfortune by her misdeeds!

Get in the way of her own happiness, indeed. What rot!

Then her heart turned cold.

"Yes, the engagement will be of short duration if I have my way," came Philip's cheerful voice, "and then we will be married."

No. No, it could not be.

Laughter poured through the door as Mrs. Worsley's voice said, "Married! I can hardly believe it. The Countess of Marnmouth!"

Sophia's mouth fell open. Philip—*her parents and Philip* were planning a match evidently so far along they now considered their marriage to be certain! She would not simply let this conversation continue without her.

For goodness sake, it was about her!

Throwing open the door and storming into the room, Sophia took a deep breath. "I thought a lady was given a say in her choice, or has that been decided for me as well?"

Philip had been seated beside her father but he rose swiftly, a shamefaced sort of smile on his face as he clutched his top hat.

He was smiling. Sophia could barely look at him, *the—the traitor! Had she not been perfectly clear?* And not just to him, but to her parents, those who should have understood her better than almost anyone!

After her two failed matches, Sophia had made it abundantly clear she had no further wish to marry. She had a fortune of her own, enough friends and acquaintances to be entertained for the rest of her life. And what had she said to Philip?

"Look, I must go back home, or my parents will think we are engaged!"

How could she be more direct? She had told him anything more permanent than this loose understanding would simply be unacceptable to her. Even when they had made love, she had spoken of it!

"Do not concern yourself, this is hardly a proposal. I am hardly ignorant of your other women."

"How—how are you even think to make such a match without my consent?" she spluttered into the silent room.

Mrs. Worsley had clearly been the one pacing. As Sophia had stormed in, she had been standing by the window and was looking at her daughter in utter astonishment.

Evidently, Sophia thought bitterly, *it was incomprehensible she would not wish for such a match.*

Philip was looking between her father and mother in surprise, as though expecting them to explain this strange turn of events. Sophia had to bite her lip to prevent herself from shouting. *This was intolerable!*

Mr. Worsley rolled his eyes as he stayed seated on the sofa. "Really, Sophia."

"Do excuse us, my lord," said Mrs. Worsley hastily, pacing across the room to grab her daughter's arm and pull her away from the gentlemen before she hissed, "He is an *earl!*"

"He is indeed," said Sophia in a clear voice. "And not my husband, if I have anything to say about it."

Where had this fury come from, pouring through her veins? Why did it hurt so much?

Philip was staring in confusion, and Sophia wanted to cry; it was all so painful. Yes, she loved him, but this was not what she wanted, and he should have known that. *Why, oh why had he not said something to her before?*

"What do you think you are doing, even thinking about refusing him?"

Her mother's whisper carried, but it did not

matter. Sophia did not care what Philip heard anymore. He had lost the right to privacy when he had come, not to her, but to her parents to demand her hand in marriage, as though she was some sort of possession to be passed between them.

"I cannot refuse him," said Sophia bitterly, "as he has not actually asked me for my hand."

Philip took a step forward, concern on his face. "I think I was quite clear when—"

"How can you have been if I am in doubt?" Sophia snapped. "No, you were not clear, because when we—we agreed it did not mean—you have made me no offer, and if you had, I would certainly have refused it!"

Her heart was still racing for reasons she could barely understand. The idea of being engaged to Philip, of marrying him…if Sophia was honest with herself, it was rather thrilling. *But he had not asked her.* There had been no profession of love, no sharing of emotions and desires.

Were two broken engagements not sufficient evidence to prove that she just wanted it to be simple? But no, he had to go behind her back. He did not understand her at all.

"Your parents and I are in agreement," Philip began in what he evidently thought was a conciliatory tone.

All it did was stoke the fires of Sophia's irritation further. "But I do not agree! I do not consent, and no amount of buttering up my parents, of going behind my back in such an ungentlemanly manner will change that!"

The pain on his face caused a twinge of guilt in Sophia's own heart, but she pushed it aside. She had not acted wrongly. She had not, despite all opportunity to speak about his serious intentions, simply ignored all decorum.

For once in her life, she was going to speak, and everyone was going to listen.

"Do not concern yourself, your lordship," said her father bracingly. "Sophia is a tad rebellious, to be sure, but she can be brought in line."

Never before had Sophia felt so incensed. *The cheek of it!* She was standing right here, and yet they continued to speak of her as though she were some child, just waiting to be raised correctly.

"If you really thought that, then perhaps you should have brought me in line years ago," Sophia snapped. "But you know it is not the truth. I *am* rebellious, if by rebellious you mean I know my own mind and am confident enough to speak it!"

"Really, Sophia," her mother attempted in a calming tone, but Sophia would not listen.

She would not be calmed. Not until people started actually heeding her words.

"And I know that confidence to speak one's mind is something most gentleman cannot stand!" Sophia said fiercely.

Philip had betrayed her in the most unconscionable way; she could not bear the sight of him. Her words had never stumbled; she had not attempted to be coy—unless that was what he thought? Unless Philip had misread her meaning, thought she was coquettishly teasing him.

No, surely not. Surely he could not be so blind?

Sophia took a deep breath. This conversation had to end, and it would end on her terms.

"Philip—Marnmouth, if you had bothered to come to me directly, speaking of your…your intentions," Sophia said with difficulty, focused on his boots rather than his face, "then I may have considered it. But as it is—"

"As it is?" Hurt sounded in his voice, and Sophia's gaze darted to his face, which was pained, his brow furrowed in genuine confusion. "Are you—do you mean to say you are going to refuse me?"

"No, no, nothing of the sort," said Mrs. Worsley hastily, turning to the gentleman. "I do not think that is what Sophia meant—*was it, Sophia?*"

Mr. Worsley had risen to his feet, the last to do so, with a stern look at his daughter. "Exactly," he said quietly. "You will say yes, won't you, Sophia?"

Sophia swallowed. "I will not."

Her voice shook.

"I have experienced engagements before. All three of you know this," she said quietly. The softness of her words seemed to calm them, and no one sought to interrupt her. "I have seen how disappointing they are. I will not engage myself to anyone, not even an earl, for the pure satisfaction of my parents. It must be my choice, if it ever occurs at all."

Silence fell after her pronouncement, and then—

"Sophia," said Philip, taking another step toward her. "I…I know you fear engagements. You have no reason to trust them, but I think you have some reason to trust me, and I would never—the idea of breaking off an engagement with—"

"You think you are the first to say such things?" Sophia asked. *Was he really this foolish?* "You really think they did not say the same things? You think these placatory notes have not been sung before? You think you are *special* in some way?"

"Yes—yes, I do!" Philip's eyes blazed as he stepped forward again, and Sophia retreated to keep distance between them.

Sophia heaved a sigh and shook her head. "Why? Why, Philip?"

This was it. This was the moment that he

could have taken the entire conversation in a different direction.

Sophia could see on his face what Philip wanted to say. He wanted to say he loved her, or some such nonsense, but by his lingering silence, it soon became clear he could not bring himself to say it in front of her parents.

In a way, that made it all the worse.

Her pride had been hurt by his decision to ignore her feelings and speak to her parents directly, but even when he had the chance to speak loving words, to make declarations, he did not.

He would not.

"I think," said Sophia in a cold voice, "it is best if you leave."

Philip's gaze darted to each of her parents in turn, but he found no help.

"I would go, your lordship," Mr. Worsley said quietly. "There will be no getting sense out of her now."

Sophia had not believed it possible to be more incensed. "Yes, because a woman speaking her mind is automatically nonsense! Stay or go then Philip, if you want to. I have nothing more to say to you."

Without waiting for a response, she turned on her heels, stormed upstairs, paying no heed to the shouts of her parents, and threw herself onto the bed.

It had all gone wrong. She had not known precisely where it had been going, whatever it was between her and Philip, but he had broken her trust, and now it was all wrong—and it was all his fault.

CHAPTER SIXTEEN

PHILIP COLLAPSED ON the sofa in the drawing room of his Mayfair townhouse. He thought furiously about the injustice of life, the idiocy of his actions, and whether or not the invention of time travel would permit him to alter the course of his life.

Well, that was a complete disaster.

The long ride to London from Bath had given him plenty of time to consider every thought that had led him to his decision, and even now, lying here utterly exhausted, he could not understand it.

He had been so clever, he had thought. *So clever.* Yet with the beauty of hindsight to guide him, he could not imagine his conversation with Sophia's parents going any worse.

Philip punched a cushion and felt much better for it.

Just when he was congratulating himself on

his cunning plan—of course, go to the parents first! Ensure they were happy with his suit so that when he spoke to Sophia, she could be reassured that he had sought her parents' permission.

Damn fool. He should have known better than that.

His visions of Sophia stepping into the room and finding, to her utter joy, that everything between them had been organized and resolved had fallen by the wayside as he endured her wrath.

"I have experienced engagements before, all three of you know this. I have seen how disappointing they are. I will not engage myself to anyone, not even an earl, for the pure satisfaction of my parents. It must be my choice if it ever occurs at all."

His good-heartened intentions—to avoid, in short, the nonsense of wedding planning—had been utterly lost; he could see that now.

He had just wanted to get it all agreed. Ever since hearing Braedon talking about her in that ridiculous way, Philip had found his heart broken.

Sophia. She had endured so much. Why would he not wish to reduce that pain, wipe away her tears, make her happy? *Make her his wife.*

He had thought she would leap at the chance. Philip punched a cushion again, and a third time for good measure. *Foolish, idiot, ignorant jape that he was!*

Just when happiness was there, Sophia had

wrenched it away. Perhaps rightly so. Maybe he did not deserve her.

Philip rose and helped himself to a large whiskey. It was what he needed after such a frosty reception and then a chilling ride back to London.

It was ironic, really, he thought as he dropped back onto the sofa. Forty years on this earth, and he had never seriously considered looking for a wife. There had always been a woman ready to accept his advances and his money, as long as she had no other expectations.

Now the boot was on the other foot. Sophia had taken the pleasure from his bones and now wished to have nothing more to do with him.

Philip tipped the glass back and allowed the amber liquid to flow down his throat, warming him and shocking him back into life.

No wonder he had had mistresses for so long— they were a far sight easier to manage than a wife! One knew where one stood with mistresses.

"I am not to be bought. Nor taken in."

"Not interested in being a mistress, then. What about a wife?"

His jaw clenched. He could not have made her his mistress. Some ladies were born to be spinsters, some to be mistresses, but others…they were destined to be wives.

Sophia was not the mistress type. She deserved to be his wife, the woman you held onto, savoring her presence, *every evening taking her to your bedchamber…*

Philip gripped his whiskey glass unnecessarily tight. *She was the woman he wanted.*

He would try again. There would be some way, he was sure, that he could help Sophia to see reason, to see his perspective on the matter.

"If you really thought that, then perhaps you should have brought me in line years ago. But you know it is not the truth. I am rebellious, if by rebellious you mean I know my own mind and am confident enough to speak it!"

Groaning into the dark silence of the room, the fire throwing up shadows, Philip closed his eyes as he took another swig of whiskey.

What a disaster.

Well, there was no point in dwelling on it. He was exhausted, every muscle in his body aching from the ride, and his mind simply could not untangle the mess of the thoughts and emotions swirling around his brain.

He opened his eyes. This was not the drawing room where he had bedded her. That was far away.

Sophia was far away.

Right now, the best thing he could do was take a long, hot bath, and then go to bed. Perhaps things would look bright in the morning. *He did not see how, but…*

His whiskey glass emptied, Philip placed it on

the table beside him.

"You look terrible."

The voice was low, but there was some mirth Philip did not take kindly to.

Only then did he realize the mere presence of the voice should give him concern. It had emanated from the shadows of the drawing room, but—*there was no one else here.*

A giggle followed, and Philip sighed heavily. Just when he was sure things could not become any worse…

Emma Tilbury rose from the armchair thrust into shadows near the back of the room.

"My, my," she said lightly with a knowing smile. "Look at what happens when I do not take care of you. You look like you could do with a release."

Philip shook his head. Emma could always be depended on to think of one thing only.

"Emma," he said, rising to his feet only to fill his glass with more whiskey. As he sat, he continued, "What in God's name are you doing here?"

There was a smile on her face as she stepped toward him and, though she did not take the seat beside him, her choice of seating was no less fortuitous, taking the armchair opposite him.

Philip took a sip of the whiskey—a little, not too much. He would need his wits about him if Emma had decided to break into his home.

"I am almost certain my servants would not have permitted you entry, particularly as they had no idea I was going to be here tonight."

Emma tilted her head to one side, examined him for a moment, and then raised a hand and placed it over her breasts, moving her gown aside to free them.

"Good God, Emma, not now—"

But it was not a display of her physical beauty she was revealing. No, Emma's hands moved back and her gown was still covering her—and there was a key entangled in those delightful fingers.

It was with a slightly abashed look that she said, "I still have a key."

Philip held his hand out. "I thought I had taken your key away from you."

Emma's smile was captivating. If he had been any other gentleman, then he would have been in real danger. As it was, Sophia's parting words were still ringing in his mind.

"I think it is best if you leave."

"You did," Emma said as she leaned forward, ensuring he had a very good look as she handed the key over. "I had a few copies made, I am sure you don't mind."

"I do very much mind," said Philip mildly. Despite seeing far more of Emma than most gentlemen could ever dream of, she simply did not stir him. His body was not interested. "And I would appreciate it if you would be honest with me and tell me whether this is the last copy you have."

Something had changed between them. He had always restrained himself from that well-worn path since he put Emma aside, but now his manhood did not even twitch.

It was Sophia; it had to be. She was the reason he just didn't see Emma the same way.

Sophia had supplanted all others in his heart, damnit, and now he had lost her.

"Almost the last one," said Emma, leaning back in her chair with a thoughtful look. "But why should I return them to you? For all I know, I may need one of them again soon."

Philip almost hung his head in his hands. Why had he lost his ability to make himself understood by the ladies?

"For the last time, Emma, it is over between us," he said seriously. "I cannot be plainer. I cannot give you the assurances you want, for I have met—it is not possible."

Philip coughed and took another swig of his drink in an attempt to distract her from his momentary slip, but Emma was not that stupid. Her intelligence had been one of the reasons he had been so attracted to her in the first place.

"In all seriousness, Philip, you look awful. I have not seen you look this unhappy since…a long time," she said, the flirtatious lilt in her voice gone. "We have been…well, friends of a sort of a long time. Tell me. What has happened?"

It was on the tip of his tongue to tell her to leave—to force her to leave him to his misery. But Philip hesitated. *Emma Tilbury had been his mistress for what, six years? Seven?*

It was hard to ignore that intimacy, even if it no longer existed. Of all the people in the world, other than Sophia, Emma understood him best.

But he could not just speak it, for he was too ashamed of his part.

"Two glasses," he said with a wry smile.

Emma's face broke into a grin. It had been the code between them, all those years ago, that they were about to have a conversation so gripping, so meaningful, it would require a glass of wine in their hands to truly enjoy it.

She moved elegantly across the room and pulled out a bottle of wine from the sideboard and two glasses, carrying them over to the fireplace. "Do you have a corkscrew?"

Philip grinned. "You don't have one of those down your bodice, do you?"

Emma stuck her tongue out. "That is in my other dress."

"Second drawer to the right, still."

There was something so comforting having Emma back in the house, he had to admit. She knew him well, yes, but she knew the house, too. If only he had been able to put his scruples aside, they could have had a very happy life together. *God's teeth, he could have married her.*

Not that he would have. It was one of the few topics they had never discussed. Emma's barrenness had made her useful as a mistress, but it would not do for the Earl of Marnmouth's wife to be unable to provide him with heirs.

As she expertly uncorked the deep red wine and poured it into two glasses, Philip sighed and tried to get his head straight.

He would tell the tale, and then Emma could be gone. He did not have to tell her the whole truth, after all. No one wanted to admit to one's old mistress that one was struggling to land a wife.

"Here you go."

Philip took the wine glass.

Emma held the second in a toast as she sat back down. "Your health, Marnmouth."

He mirrored her, toasting her health, and saw that broad smile he knew so well.

Miserable as he was, it was impossible not to feel guilty. She loved him in her own way. She wanted him, at the very least, despite the fact he had put her aside ages ago. It was sad, really. She wanted him, and he wanted Sophia, and neither were getting what they wanted.

Emma sipped the wine. "Your cellar always was the best in London. 'Tis those Devonshire pirates you keep hush about."

Philip laughed. "Something like that."

"So. Which woman has upset you?"

He raised an eyebrow. "What makes you think 'tis a lady?"

It was a foolish thing to say, and he knew it, but he could not help it.

No wonder Emma laughed. "Oh, Marnmouth, just when I think you are a sensible man. Be truthful now. No gentleman has ever affected you in this way. Remember, I was your favorite mistress for a long time, but you had others in between. I know what a rebellious lady who will not play your games does to you."

Philip shifted uncomfortably in his seat. Just when he thought he would have a quiet evening, he had to find himself with one of the sharpest women in London. *Too bad she also knew him far too well.*

"Fine, I will tell you all, though there is little to say and even less to celebrate," he said, attempting an airy tone as he swallowed some wine. "I have met a young lady that I like. More than like, I suppose. And despite wooing her, courting her—"

"Bedding her?"

Despite her words, Emma had a most angelic look on her face, and as she sipped her wine and watched him closely, she laughed.

Damn and blast it. He should not have hesitated. He should have just lied!

"Well done, sir," she said in a mocking tone.

"Very impressive. And a lady, too, which was far more than I was when you first took me to bed."

Philip sighed. *No gentleman should have to endure this.* "The long and short of it is, I made an offer to her parents, she overheard and thought I was going behind her back—I was only asking permission, of a kind!"

Even he could hear his petulance. *Christ alive, he was more child than man.*

Emma was shaking her head. "You should have come straight to me."

That was it. He would have to put his foot down—could a man not complain to his mistress about his difficulties landing a wife without her throwing herself at him again?

"I am not going back, Emma. I have to go forward, and we had our time," Philip said, the whiskey and wine loosening his tongue, stripping it of all pleasantries. "God in his Heaven, I have always been clear about this, and it is time you heeded my words. I am not going to simply run back to you every time I…"

His voice trailed away as he saw her look of genuine hurt. *Christ and all the devils.*

"I meant," she said tartly, "you should have come to me for *advice*. If anyone can help you secure the lady of your choice, 'tis I. After all, I am the perfect person for this—I know you better than anyone, and I am a lady myself. Of sorts."

Philip laughed despite himself. "I am not sure

whether I would ever describe you as a lady, Emma."

She grinned. "Well, maybe not. But did it even occur to you to speak with Miss Sophia Worsley yourself, before you went to her parents, cap in hand?"

It was fortunate he had not been taking another sip of wine at that moment, for he would have spilled the dark crimson liquid all down his white linen shirt.

How did—he had never mentioned Sophia's name, had he? Philip quickly ran back through their conversation as best he could. No, he did not recall saying either Sophia or Worsley. *So how on earth…*

"Tut, tut, you are starting to lose your touch," said Emma. "'Tis almost like you have forgotten what it is to gossip! Come on, Philip, you honestly do not think anything happens in society without the world knowing about it?"

Philip swallowed. *Ah. Of course.* Yes, they had been seen in public more than once, and since the entire Worsley family had dined with him at Camden Place…

"Though I admit," said Emma softly, "the fact that you have bedded her was news I had not heard."

Heat seared through his body. "Emma, I warn you, you must not tell anyone I said—if Sophia's reputation—"

"Do not concern yourself, you foolish man. I know you are far more interested in her reputation than you ever were about mine."

Philip tried to think. Emma was trustworthy, he was sure of that. Besides, she owed him far more than she could ever repay.

Years ago he had found her in a brothel, and not the most savory of types. It had been his first venture into one, tired as he was by the mistresses he could acquire through serving girls, and there she had been. *Emma Tilbury.*

He was almost certain that was not her actual name, but it was the name she had given, and when he had bought her from her madam, she had kept it.

After installing her as his mistress in an apartment, showering her with jewels, gowns, and invitations to the houses of the great and the good, they had reveled together in rebelling against the world.

He had done more for her than he had ever done for anyone, now he came to think about it.

If only he had been kinder. This close, he could see what the ravages of years without his protection have wrought. Emma looked...tired. There were a few wrinkles around her eyes which had not been there six months ago, and her gown that subtly clung to her well-formed body was cheap. She had pawned her silks.

"Let me talk to her."

Philip started. "No—*no*, absolutely not."

Emma was smiling. "I can talk sense into her, this Miss Worsley. After all, I know how good you are in bed."

Well, Sophia would certainly not listen to him, and her parents she was evidently going to ignore...

Philip sighed and drained his wine glass. "I need to do this alone—and I need to be alone. I think this means goodnight, Emma."

She looked disappointed. "You are alone. I hardly count, surely."

"Yes, you do," he said gently. "We may not be...we may not have an association anymore, but you are still a person, and in my eyes, you will always be a lady. Come on, I am throwing you out."

The last sentence was said bracingly as he rose to his feet. He had no wish to manhandle her out of the place, of course. He was depending on her to follow his suit.

Emma sighed, drained her wine glass impressively, and set it down.

"You always were the gentleman," she said, rising to her feet.

And then she was kissing him, had closed the gap between them, and locked her lips with his. He could taste the wine on her lips, smell the fragrance of a cheap scent, and it was Emma, the woman he had known for most of his life...

And yet, it was not enough. He felt nothing.

She was not Sophia.

Emma broke the kiss and looked him closely in the eyes. "Well?"

Philip shrugged helplessly. "Nothing. I am sorry, Emma."

She looked at him in the most strange way, and then she smiled. "Nothing for me either. How strange. It appears we have finally managed to cut ties. You must really love her."

It did not occur to Philip to inquire whether she had found someone else before the door shut behind her and he was alone.

Blast. Cold, alone, and unhappy. *Was this truly to be his lot?*

CHAPTER SEVENTEEN

WHEN THE CARRIAGE jostled Sophia into the window, she did not try to hold herself steady. Her head tapped into the window, but she ignored the pain radiating through her temple.

What did it matter? What was the point in fighting the movement of the carriage on its long road back to London?

What, in short, was the use in preventing physical pain when everything within her ached with unhappiness?

There was a loud sniff. Sophia lifted up her head just enough to take in her mother, seated opposite her. Mrs. Worsley had a lace handkerchief held up to her face and was sniffing into it loudly, all in her continued attempt to demonstrate to her daughter just how upset she was by her betrayal.

Not agreeing to marry an earl, it appeared,

was a great treachery and was not easily to be forgiven, or at least that was what her mother had shouted at her the evening before.

Sophia sighed. *There was no point in saying anything.* Trees rushed past the windows as the carriage jolted along the well-worn path from Bath to London. There were many other carriages on the road, but they were all going in the opposite direction.

The Season would be beginning soon, and the best of society would be arriving, ready to spend their guineas in the best shops to ensure they were correctly attired.

Not the Worsleys. No, Sophia was being taken back to London in disgrace. That had been the primary cause of the row that morning.

Philip. Sophia forced down the rising emotions the mere memory of his name accorded and focused on the rushing world.

She had no wish to return to London, and not just because she was now sure to miss the Bath operas she loved so much. But her father had been resolute.

"We are going back to London, and that is the last I will say of the matter," Mr. Worsley had barked that morning. "No, I tell you, Sophia, you have lost all rights to dictate matters to myself and your mother. If you had only been reasonable, been *obedient*, then you would have had higher precedence. As it is, we are going back home."

"I do not see why we must quit our rooms here," Mrs. Worsley had said, breakfast forgotten as the three Worsley bickered. "My friends will be arriving and—"

"No!" Sophia's father had slammed his hands onto the table in a rare show of irritation, taking a moment to calm his breathing before continuing. "The carriage is ordered, our trunks are packed. We are going."

The carriage jerked as it turned around a corner. Even her mother's ministrations had been insufficient to calm her father's anger at her refusal, and so they were leaving.

"What is the point in staying, Mariah?" she had overheard her father say bitterly as she left the breakfast room. "We only came to find a husband for Sophia, and she has made it quite clear she does not want one. So. London."

The sound of quiet crying had drifted through the open door into the hallway, and Sophia had felt tears prickle in her own eyes. She had never wanted to make her mother cry. She had never wanted to disappoint, offend, or anger her parents—but what could she say?

She would not marry a man who did not even have the common decency to come and speak to her about his intentions. Asking permission, that was different. *But just assuming that it was all agreed before a word was spoken to her?*

She did not want to marry Philip. She *did* want to marry Philip. Like a pendulum, she swung, unable to maintain her opinion for more than one minute together.

His face floated before her memory. Handsome, charming—but that did not excuse him. She had shared some of her closest thoughts, her deepest fears with him…and he had not heeded. If he had, he would have known not to just stride over to her parents, impress them with his title, and demand her like some sort of chattel!

Philip had not said he loved her. He had not asked her to marry him. *He had plotted with her parents to marry her off, like an—an embarrassment!*

The carriage jerked as it tipped around a corner, and Sophia's forehead tapped on the window again. The pain echoed how she felt inside.

She glanced at her father, who was seated beside her mother. Mr. Worsley had not spoken to his daughter since they had entered the carriage yesterday morning and probably wouldn't until they were back in London.

He avoided her gaze.

Sophia bit her lip. It was evident her father was still offended, angry with her for refusing to marry the Earl of Marnmouth.

She was sorry for it, but not sorry enough to apologize. She had acted as her heart had seen fit; something her parents had always instilled in her.

She had done nothing wrong! It was no crime to refuse to marry a gentleman, even one as handsome, wealthy, and respected as Philip.

"Sophia, I…I know you fear engagements for natural reasons. You have no reason to trust them, but I think you have some reason to trust me, and I would never—the idea of breaking off an engagement with—"

Sophia closed her eyes. Just a few more hours, and she could be released from this prison and avoid her parents. Perhaps she should take a house separately from them—maybe ask Harry whether she could stay with them for a while. She was fully grown, after all. She could not live with her parents forever.

Mrs. Worsley gave a hearty sniff, and Sophia rolled her eyes. *My word, but they were both as bad as each other.* Did they think their dramatic displeasure would encourage her to suddenly decide to accept Philip's advances?

They were foolish if they thought Philip would even want to offer for her again. Sophia had seen the hurt in his eyes as she had ordered him to leave. He would never forgive her.

Not that she wanted him to. *Did she?*

Desperate to force her mind away from Philip, engagements, marriages, and all the pain and confusion those topics raised, Sophia reached into her reticule and pulled out one of the few books she had brought to Bath in her hasty packing to chase after Philip.

She was attempting not to think of him! Opening the book, Sophia attempted to read.

She had never seen such a house before. Tall towers spiked against the sky as heavy clouds clustered around its spires, dark shadows throwing the gargoyles into terrifying relief…

Sophia swallowed. Each of those words individually made sense, to be sure, but as a group, she could not comprehend them.

She had never seen Philip's seat in Devon, and now she never would.

Sophia closed the book angrily and looked out of the window. *How was it possible for Philip to intrude into all her thoughts, no matter what she did?* It was most unfair.

He had pierced her heart when no other gentlemen ever had. But love was not enough. It had to be paired with so many other things—respect, for a start. If Philip had respected her, he would have spoken to her first. Sophia had never been in love before, never known the painful sting it could create when it was unheeded or unrequited.

And it was unrequited. Philip had never said anything about his feelings, even when he had stood there before her parents. And what had he said? *Nothing.*

"If you had just agreed to marry the earl, we would be planning your wedding!"

It was her father who had exploded into the

silence, and Sophia could not help but laugh dryly. *Clearly, she was not the only one thinking angrily of the last few days, but she was not going to give in now. They could not force her to marry anyone.*

"What would be the point?" she said sarcastically. "We've planned two weddings!"

Mrs. Worsley sniffed into her handkerchief.

Sophia sighed. "Mother, 'tis not the end of the world! I will live with the two of you, happily, or find other arrangements if that better suits all parties!"

"Other...other arrangements?" said her mother faintly.

"I do not understand this constant desire to marry me off. I need no fortune, no man to tell me what to do. I can spend the rest of my life doing whatever I wish, choosing only to make myself happy. What woman would not want such a life?"

Her father disagreed. "A rebel, then, right to the end. I think it disgraceful—a disgrace on the whole family!"

Irritation flared in Sophia's heart. "If a woman doing what she wants is a rebel, then, yes, I am one."

It was enough to make her a bluestocking, the way her parents were acting. *Had they no dreams? Did they not wish for more than simply doing what she was told?*

A quick glance through the window made

Sophia's shoulders sag with relief. *Hammersmith.* They were close to London, and, in just a little while, she would escape this stifling carriage and leave her parents to stew in their misery.

Could they not see that the world was changing— that she had changed?

Robert had been nice enough, and Jacob had been a source of respectability. Philip could have been…

Well, he was no longer an option. Sophia steeled her heart against him and knew she could never see him again.

Twenty minutes later, the Worsley carriage rattled down their street, and Sophia opened the door before the carriage stopped moving.

"Careful!" called Mrs. Worsley.

Sophia ignored her. *Careful? She had been careful all her life, and where had that got her? Almost nowhere.*

Stepping lightly onto the street, Sophia thanked God they had arrived. Instead of stepping toward their front door, Sophia walked in the opposite direction.

"Sophia? Sophia?"

She ignored her mother's words. Her pelisse around her shoulders would keep her warm in the chilly air, and she had a great desire to walk in any direction but that of home.

"Sophia, where are you going?"

"I do not know," she snapped to her father.

All she wanted to do was walk and put distance between them. *The more distance, the better.*

As she turned the corner, the shouts of her parents disappeared. Despite the chill in the air, she was hot, anger keeping her far warmer than any pelisse could. *Besides, the pain she felt was still deep within her heart.*

Sophia forced her way past people on the pavement without giving them a second glance. Philip, knowing how she felt about matrimony, about the whole foolish circus, knowing how she had been hurt again and again—what had possessed him to go to her parents with such a ridiculous plan?

Sophia's unconscious footsteps guided her to one of her favorite places in the city, Hyde Park. There was a cooling breeze rustling the trees, and it was welcome after her rushed break away from her parents. Walking slowly in the gardens, it was finally possible for the tension in her shoulders to start to dissipate.

Sophia sighed. *She could not stay here forever.* At some point, she would have to return home and face her parents—and attempt to explain this was no childish tantrum. It had been a serious breach of her privacy for them to concoct her future with no thought of her whatsoever.

Yet, he had wanted her. Sophia had seen it in his eyes, though his lips had spoken nothing of it. True, their lovemaking had been no proposal…

"Do not concern yourself, this is hardly a proposal. I am hardly ignorant of your other women."

Just as her thoughts wandered back to Philip and that heady night, the sensation of his arms around her, someone actually grabbed her arm.

"Miss Worsley?"

Sophia pulled away instinctively. "How dare you touch…" Her voice trailed away. She had turned and found herself looking into the eyes of none other than…

"Miss Tilbury," she said coldly, bobbing a short curtsey before walking away.

"You are Miss Worsley, then?"

Sophia tried to ignore the voice and forced down a most unladylike retort. *The last person she wished to speak to in this moment, other than Philip, was his mistress!*

"Do not concern yourself, I am not offended," came Miss Tilbury's voice from behind her. "I would not wish to speak with me, either."

Sophia's footsteps slowed until she stopped. It was impossible not to. Despite herself, compassion poured through her bones.

Were they that different, really? In a strange way, they had both loved and lost the same man. *How was it possible to love and hate the same man?* Marriage had never truly been on the cards, she was sure of it, and for him to go behind her back…

Sophia swallowed. "What do you want from

me?"

Miss Tilbury was wearing a gentleman's greatcoat, warm and fur-lined for the winter, but it did not fit her well, and she appeared a little swallowed by it. Still, it was possible to see her great beauty and why Philip had cared for so long.

"'Tis more what I can do for you if I am honest," said Miss Tilbury with a knowing smile. "Come. Walk with me."

She started to walk sedately down the path, but Sophia hesitated.

This was all most irregular. How had Miss Tilbury known she was here, or was it a coincidence? Why would she want to speak with her lover's previous mistress? She could not imagine the woman had much to say she did not already know.

And yet, curiosity filled her heart. Miss Tilbury had approached her, knowing Sophia would more likely than not ignore her. *Why risk it?*

Sophia walked quickly to reach Miss Tilbury.

After a few moments, the older woman said, "You have done something fascinating to Philip, you know. Something quite unique, I commend you."

A backhanded compliment? "I have no idea what you are talking about."

"I mean it in all seriousness," said Miss Tilbury quietly as they stepped along the path. "I have never seen him like this before. You have bewitched him somehow, taken all of his true attention, his true feelings. I almost feel as though *you* have seduced *him*, rather than the other way around."

Despite herself, Sophia laughed. "Me? I never feel in control when I am with him, that's all I know."

Her cheeks burned. It felt wanton to speak this way, but then how would anyone else understand but another woman who had encountered Philip at his best?

Miss Tilbury was nodding. "I completely comprehend you—and please, do not misunderstand my intentions by approaching you like this. I am not here to make you discomforted. I wish to help."

"And I, in my turn, will be honest and say that I have no desire to speak with Philip's mistress," Sophia said stiffly. *This was the most unnerving conversation she had ever had!*

But she was apparently not alone in that.

Miss Tilbury stopped and glared. "I am my own person, not just Philip's old mistress."

Her words were spoken so fiercely that Sophia swallowed. It was true, she had just considered her some part of Philip's past, but she was her own person. *Were not all ladies merely described as so and so's daughter, or the wife of Mr. Whomever?*

"You are right, and I apologize. I am…there are many things I am still learning. I assume you have spoken with me today because you have—well, words of wisdom for me?"

Miss Tilbury's hair was tugged by a gust of wind as she tilted her head to examine her. Sophia felt a little self-conscious by her piercing gaze. *What was she thinking?*

"Ignore me, all thoughts of me, entirely," said Miss Tilbury suddenly. "Think of him. Philip. How do you feel?"

Sophia closed her eyes. There were so many conflicting emotions in her heart, it was almost impossible to untangle them.

"Wretched. In pain. Lost. Like…like something is missing."

As she opened her eyes, she saw Miss Tilbury was nodding. "Yes, I thought so. 'Tis because you are not with him. You should be."

"You—you do not know me!" retorted Sophia with a little feeling.

Miss Tilbury smiled. "But I know him, and I can tell you now, he is feeling much the same. Remind me again why the two of you fools have turned your backs on love?"

CHAPTER EIGHTEEN

*T*HIS WAS A *damned nuisance, discovering he cared about the woman!*

If he had felt nothing for Sophia Worsley, he would not be standing like an absolute nincompoop waiting for her, his heart pumping more than blood and panic around his body.

He had never felt like this before. No lady had ever managed to sear into his heart like Sophia, even Emma.

No, he had been confident amongst the ladies. Why else had he managed to bed so many of them? *But now…what was the world coming to? What was his world coming to?*

Philip smiled despite his fluttering heart. Sophia had changed his world. It would never be the same, and that was why he was here—to see whether he could put the world to right and have Sophia back in his arms, where she belonged.

Philip's nose curled at the heady scents pouring through Almack's. Everyone seemed to be wearing entirely different fragrances, merging and mixing in the air like a heady poison.

His senses were pricked for any sign of Sophia, and instead, they were under assault by every wile of the ladies looking to nab him for their daughters. Philip smiled weakly at one particular matron who had passed him several times, each time with a different daughter, as though ascertaining which would attract him best.

"I hate Almack's," said Larnwick heavily. "God, I wish I was in Scotland. I have no idea how you manage to stand it, Marnmouth. I really don't."

Philip nodded mechanically. Larnwick had been talking for a good while, and, as long as Philip nodded every now and again, the man did not require him to input.

Really, Almack's was more cattle market now than dancehall! But still, Sophia would be here. She had to be.

Philip paid little attention to the gossip pages—crucial when one's mistress was splattered all over them—but knew the Worsleys had returned to London, and that surely meant a return to Almack's. After all, when one did not attend Almack's and the matrons of the establishment knew, you had essentially snubbed the place.

Snub Almack's, lose your voucher.

Philip took a deep breath and shuffled his feet again. And it was most important that Sophia attended Almack's tonight because…

Damnit, he was going to propose.

"Sometimes I wish I had never done it," Larnwick was saying in a low voice. "Propose, I mean. For God's sake, it was years ago, and if I had known what I know now…"

It was a foolish scheme, and one Philip was certain would go afoul, but he had to do it. If not for Sophia's sake, then for his conscience. It was what he should have done in the first place, he could see now. *If only it had been so obvious when he had had the chance!*

Though she was likely to decline him, and publicly, too, which would be humiliating, he had to ask. He had to be certain in his heart he had done everything in his power to win her.

She was everything. Sophia was all he wanted out of this life, and to leave a little for his daughters.

In the days since he had returned to London, Philip had already attempted to make amends. As soon as he had heard the Worsleys had unaccountably returned to London after taking their rooms in Bath early for this Season, he had gone to their home.

Sophia had not seen him. She had not even permitted him to take one step into the house, as a tearful Mrs. Worsley had explained. Mr.

Worsley had not spoken, just stood behind his wife with his head low.

Philip was certain the three Worsleys would make an appearance at Almack's. Life turned out to be utterly intolerable without her.

"Engagements are a trap for the weak, I must say that, Marnmouth," said Larnwick heavily. "I had thought myself besotted—in a way, I suppose I was. But really…"

The noisy, smoky rooms of Almack's were not the hazy and pleasure-filled splendor that they had once been. Philip looked out at the crowds and saw few people he actually recognized, which was a shame.

He sighed heavily as his gaze moved through the crowd, seeking out the face of the one person who could bring a skip to his heart.

"—and Miss Lymington is simply not the woman I had thought," said Larnwick with a shake of his head.

Philip snapped back to attention. He had not contributed to the conversation for a while now. *Poor old Larnwick could not be expected to keep it going all on his own.*

"Ah, yes, the Lymingtons," he said aloud. "There are quite a few of them, from what I understand, and you are engaged to one of the twins? Ah, yes, I can see them over there."

He pointed at the gaggle of Lymingtons congregated on the other side of the room.

For some inexplicable reason, Larnwick sighed. "Oh, hell, why did you have to point them—yes, they have seen me. Now I have no excuse not to speak with them—rot in hell, Marnmouth."

The Scotsman stalked away, leaving Philip utterly confused. *Surely he could not have said or done anything to truly injure the man?*

"What on earth did you say to Larnwick?"

Braedon walked over to Philip, with a raised eyebrow, and Chester.

Philip shrugged. "You know, I have no idea. Do you think I could have offended him? I know so few Scotsmen, I assume they are a little more delicate than us Londoners."

Chester shook his head. "You know, I do not think Larnwick has been pleasant for weeks. I can rarely get a straight answer out of the man for when he will be back in Scotland. Seems to think if he goes back, the engagement with Miss Lymington will be called off."

"What a fuss over nonsense!" grinned Braedon, glass of wine in his hand. "I think he is naught but tired over the whole venture, and that is where his ill-temper comes from. You know I have heard they are going to release one hundred white doves outside the church?"

His laughter was joined by that of Chester. "What nonsense! Truly, one hundred?"

The conversation continued, but Philip did

not partake. His gaze sweeping across the halls of Almack's—all in search of one face. *Where was Sophia?*

"—of course, the Lymingtons are desperate for the wedding, all these delays—"

There! Philip had to be careful not to cry out in excitement as he saw them. Mr. and Mrs. Worsley. They looked subdued, and, more importantly, they were alone. Sophia was not with them.

"I said, do you not agree, Marnmouth?"

Philip jumped. "What?" he said wildly, looking between his two companions.

Braedon shook his head. "You know, ever since you fell for that Worsley girl, you have been absolutely useless!"

"You are a little distracted, Marnmouth," said Chester with concern. "Are you sure you are quite well?"

But Philip had no interest for them, not now that the Worsleys had arrived. "Yes, yes, indeed," he said vaguely, walking away without a farewell greeting.

He had to speak with the Worsleys. Was Sophia at home, unwell? Had her constitution failed her? Had he, by his reckless and careless approach for her hand, caused a collapse?

It only took him a minute to cross the heaving room, and he bowed low to Mr. and Mrs. Worsley. "Madam, sir," he said abruptly.

As he straightened up, Philip saw they were embarrassed to be addressed by him. *Christ in his heaven, but they would have to accept their acquaintance was not over, surely!*

His heart leaped at the very thought that any minute now, he could ask Sophia the question that had been in his heart since he had made love to her on the furs by the fire.

He just had not realized it.

"Mr. Worsley," Philip started formally. "I wished to inquire exactly where—"

"Do not get your hopes up, your lordship," interrupted Mr. Worsley as his wife's cheeks pinked. "She is not here."

Mrs. Worsley's look of embarrassment increased. "I do apologize for my daughter, your lordship, but she is…she is indisposed."

Philip waited for more, but no words were forthcoming. "Indisposed."

"Yes, with a headache," Mrs. Worsley said hastily—*too hastily*, Philip thought. "It has plagued her for the last few days, and so has been unable to see anyone, and it was her greatest wish to be recovered enough to attend Almack's tonight, but alas…"

Her voice trailed away.

Philip attempted to marshal his thoughts. It could not be clearer the Worsleys were lying, and it was quite understandable why they should wish to do so.

So, Sophia was still avoiding him—avoiding any place she could guess he would be.

Mrs. Worsley looked mortified, whereas her husband looked merely angry. Evidently, he had not been able to persuade, cajole, or force Sophia to attend Almack's tonight.

Philip was too much of a gentleman to expose their falsehoods, however. "What a shame. I am sorry to hear Miss Worsley is so unwell," he said quietly. "I hope you will give her my best wishes for her recovery."

Mrs. Worsley caught his eye, and he saw the hurt. *This was his doing.* If he had gone straight to Sophia and engaged her affections, they would all be in Bath enjoying the Season.

As it was…

"Thank you, your lordship," said Mr. Worsley stiffly. "And now I am sure you will excuse us."

Philip watched them disappear into the swelling crowd and sighed. *What was he supposed to do now?*

Because Sophia was not ill in bed with a headache, he knew it. He knew her better than anyone! Something tied them together, a bond which had never existed before.

Philip tried to think. If Sophia had no wish to be in Almack's, it was quite natural to feign a headache—but if he knew Sophia, she would not simply stay at home to be bored.

He had a sneaking suspicion of where she would actually be, but even so, that would be very rebellious of her. Rebellious for anyone. *Still, as soon as the thought occurred to him…*

Philip started to stride toward the doors of Almack's when a hand grabbed his arm. "Where do you think you are going, Marnmouth?"

Philip turned to Braedon. "I think to find my future wife. But I am not sure. I will have to let you know."

Braedon's eyes widened. "You are not sure?"

"Not in the slightest," said Philip optimistically. "'Tis a gamble."

Braedon hesitated and then removed his hand with a nod. "Good luck, then!"

"Thank you," muttered Philip. He had become momentarily distracted by Miss Emma Tilbury, who had walked past them in one of her more splendid gowns.

Well. Cut low on the bodice to reveal far more of her than was socially acceptable.

Philip saw Braedon's eyes follow her and stifled a laugh. *Emma still had it, after all these years.*

As he stepped into the night, Philip found his heart beating rapidly. His guess was wild, certainly, and it was a gamble—and a small part of him hoped he was wrong about his surmise as to Sophia's whereabouts.

Nevertheless, he had a feeling she was more predictable than she realized.

His destination was only three streets away, and as he tapped on the door, he took a deep breath. "God save the Queen."

The door slid open and allowed the sound of angry shouting and the clatter of furniture being thrown around to rise up to the silent London street.

Philip shook his head wryly as he stepped down the corridor. *Was it an evening in the Queen of Hearts if there was not a raucous fight?*

There certainly was a disagreement going on downstairs, and that was hardly unusual—and in a strange way, it calmed him. If a lady had been present downstairs—a lady such as Sophia, for example—the proprietor would surely not permit such an outrage to continue.

A scream pierced the night, and Philip's heart went cold. *It was Sophia, he knew it.* He had heard that scream before, and his blood iced in his veins.

She was here. In the Queen of Hearts, during a fight.

Running the last few paces, Philip saw to his horror Sophia standing in the center of the room having a blazing row with a man, with what appeared to be a stolen gentleman's cane in his hand.

"—cheated me for the last time," Sophia was saying, having to shout over the din as observers jeered. "I will not leave without my money sir, and—"

Philip hastily stepped forward. "Sophia!"

Turning in utter astonishment, her mouth fell open. "Philip?"

But it was too late. The man who had apparently cheated her took advantage of her wandering eye and made a grab for her.

"Come 'ere, girly, you can pay me in more ways than one!"

All logic, all rational thought disappeared. *The idea that anyone was touching Sophia except him—worse, without her consent, in such a lewd and disgusting manner?*

Roaring like a wounded bull, Philip rushed forward without thought. His fist did the thinking. In a staggering crash, the man fell to the ground, blood spurting from his nose.

Philip was panting heavily and could barely think what he was going to do next. *The blaggard, the rogue, the pimpersnapping idiotic—*

"Ah, y'lordship," said the owner calmly, peering over the bar. "Still breathing, but out cold. I congratulate you, sir."

Philip looked up at Sophia, who was staring in wonder. It was only then that he realized she was wearing breeches again.

There was no time to think, not anymore. *Who knew how many friends the man, now lying on the floor in a pool of his own blood, had in the place?* No, they needed to get out of here fast.

Grabbing Sophia's arm despite her instant protestations, he pulled her for the third time out of the Queen of Hearts.

"Let go of me, you brute! How dare you interfere with my private—unhand me!"

They reached the street, but still, Philip did not stop pulling her along with him.

"You are the most irritating, most infuriating, most ignorant—"

Philip did not stop until they were under one of the newfangled gas streetlamps on Pall Mall, and he could take a proper look at her. His gaze raked over every inch, looking for any way that blaggard could have hurt her.

"Are you going to say anything, you, you—"

"Enough," Philip said shortly. *Her tongue was certainly unharmed, at the very least.*

Sophia looked suspicious as she pulled her arm from his grip. "What are you doing? Why are you looking at me like that?"

"I am looking for injuries."

Sophia rolled her eyes. "You are so dramatic, Philip."

"And so are you, you foolish—what did you think you were playing at, going to the Queen of Hearts *again?*" Philip snapped. His heart was still racing. *Once again, he had ridden to the rescue, and once again, she seemed utterly uncaring he had saved her!* "You could have been seriously hurt, Sophia. You told me you weren't going to go there again!"

"I also told you that I had no wish to consider marriage again, and yet you utterly ignored that!" Sophia's eyes were bright, and Philip's heart twisted.

Damn. Damn and blast, but this woman owned him, could do anything she wanted with him. If she ordered him to lie down and worship her, he would. Why couldn't she see that?

"I had no intentions of falling in love with you."

Sophia's eyes widened, and she took a step back. "You…you love me?"

Philip nodded. *Perhaps that was what she had been waiting for.* "I love you, Sophia, and I should have said so before. So there you have it. I love you, you care naught for me, and that is an end to it."

Turning away, he started to stomp down the street. *Well, he had managed to make another fool of himself. Perhaps he would go onto the Continent. Being near her…it pained him.*

A hand slipped into his own. "You love me."

Philip glanced at Sophia, who was inexplicably smiling. "Yes."

Her smile broadened. "Why did you not say so in the first place? Well, there is only one thing for it, then. We will have to wed. Immediately."

Her words made no sense. "You told me you were never going to marry," Philip reminded her.

Sophia stopped under another lamppost. "I changed my mind. We ladies can do that, you know."

Philip stared. *She could not have said what he thought he heard...could she?*

She was leaning against the lamppost now, a broad smile on her face.

"You..." said Philip weakly, and then tried again. "Are you in earnest?"

Sophia nodded. "You will have to elope with me, mark you. I have no wish for a big wedding. I do not really want a wedding at all. A *marriage* is what I want with you, Philip. We can celebrate with my parents if we really have to when we return."

Philip started to smile himself. "Let me get this right. You are proposing to me?"

She laughed, her breath blossoming into the night air. "And 'tis the only proposal between us, I may add. I had to take matters into my own hands."

He could restrain himself no longer. Stepping to close the distance between them, Philip kissed his beloved passionately, pouring all the fear that he had lost her into the kiss to ensure she knew, she had to know, just what she meant to him.

When he finally released her, Sophia's eyes were hazy with desire. "Promise me, though—we will elope tonight. Now. No big wedding."

Philip nodded. "A rebel to the last."

CHAPTER NINETEEN

S OPHIA TOOK A deep breath. There was no looking glass in the pokey, dark-beamed room she had been shown into the night before. The inn at Gretna Green, though popular, was hardly the height of luxury.

This meant she had a restless night in the creaky bed in the corner, and she was unable to view her appearance before she descended the stairs, but she did not care.

She knew what she looked like, and she knew Philip loved her.

"I love you, Sophia and I should have said so before. So there you have it. I love you, you care naught for me, and that is an end to it."

Sophia smiled. Weak sunlight was pouring through the tiny window. *Daybreak.*

It did not matter whether her hair was adequately pinned back into curls or if her gown was hanging right at the back, a constant source of irritation for her mother's lady's maid. No, Philip was not here to wed a perfect woman. He was here to wed her and not her gown, no matter how well it was tied.

Sophia shivered. And once they were married, her gown may not play a part of the rest of the day's proceedings. It was a heady, wanton thought, but she could not help it.

Stepping across the room took a mere moment, and then Sophia was peering out of the window over the small village.

Gretna Green. She had heard of it many times, but usually in the gossip pages where some shameful marriage had been hushed up and made as proper as could be. Just a small scattering of houses and buildings along the road. They had almost missed it in the dark.

Three long days on the road had soared by with Philip as a companion. Sophia could not believe hours slipped away, lost in the joys of talking, discovering more, growing in new understandings to see them through the many years of happy marriage they had ahead of them.

True, they had indulged in pleasures they probably shouldn't have, and Sophia's cheeks burned to think of them—*what a way to pass the time.*

Her eyelashes fluttered at the mere memory of what Philip could do with his tongue.

They had been less careful than they should,

that was certain. No preservatives had been packed, and still, they had enjoyed themselves, taken their indulgence again and again.

They knew where they were headed. Gretna Green, to become man and wife. *What difference did a few days make?*

Sophia's wandering gaze fell onto the smithy at the edge of the village. It was larger than any she had seen before—though that was no surprise. Smoke started to drift upward from its chimney; dark black at first, growing lighter until it was white.

Her observations were interrupted by a knock at her bedchamber door, and a broad smile crept over Sophia's face. He had evidently been watching for the smoke in his room, the tiny one he had gallantly insisted on taking last night when they had been so weary on their feet that any bed would do.

Another knock on her door echoed through the room. "Wife!"

Sophia strode over to the door and threw it open. "I am not your wife!"

Philip grinned. "Not yet."

His kiss was fierce, demanding all of her, and Sophia willingly gave it. She would give him everything, this man who had taught her not only to love but to trust again.

Her hands moved instinctively to his neck, pulling him closer, deepening the kiss, and Sophia felt her entire body shiver for the delight he gave her. *His arms were around her waist, and if she was not much mistaken…*

"Philip!" she said, laughing as she pulled away. "Leave my gown alone. It needs to stay on me—for at least a little while longer!"

Philip groaned as he looked past her to the bed. "Do you think we have time for—"

It was impossible not to laugh. "No! You need to make an honest woman of me, Philip, and then you can have your way with me as many times as you like."

There was a mischievous smile on his face as her beloved said quietly, "Promise?"

Sophia grinned. *She was going to love this man for the rest of her life.* "No. I am a rebel, and I can do whatever I want."

Philip rolled his eyes in a way that made Sophia giggle. "My goodness, you have got that from my father! Be careful. You don't want to pick up too many of his habits."

He looked genuinely surprised. "What? You are jesting—I have taken that from you!"

Sophia laughed. "What? I do not do that, 'tis a most irritating habit my father has had for years. My mother does not seem to be able to cure him. Come on."

For some inexplicable reason, Philip stared with a certain level of incredulity as Sophia took his hand and pulled him down the corridor. The staircase creaked mournfully as they descended to greet the only person already awake.

"Good morning to ye'selves," said the innkeeper with a broad grin. "And 'tis just the one bedchamber for tonight, I take it?"

Sophia felt her cheeks burn. *It was more than a little discomforting to know the whole world knew what she would be doing that evening!*

Her gaze shifted to Philip, and she felt the awkwardness melt away like snow in spring. It was obvious, then, how much they loved each other.

Anyone who made the journey to Gretna Green to arrive in the dead of night and asked for two rooms and what time the smithy opened the next morning were hardly hiding their intentions.

Before she could respond, Philip grinned. "Yes—in a few minutes, we will be man and wife!"

The innkeeper's eyes twinkled. "Aye, I thought it mebbe summat like that. Now I tell you straight, Angus is a good man, but beware to pay him well. 'Tis plenty a couple I've seen who has been stingy with their payment and found their horses unshod for the journey back!"

Sophia laughed. "Thank you, kind sir—and I must say, I do love your country. It is so wild, I feel like anything can happen."

Philip nodded, his arm tight around her. "I am a southerner through and through, but maybe

I need to take a house here. Larnwick can recommend one. You know Larnwick, Sophia?"

Before she could respond, the air was torn in twain by the heavy noise of metal hitting metal.

The innkeeper nodded sagely. "Ah, there he is. You had better hurry up, sir, miss—I think ye's the only couple today, but once Angus gets his fire up, it'll be fair boiling in there."

Sophia nodded and slipped her arm through Philip's. "Come on then, Marnmouth. Time to make an honest woman of me."

She colored for saying such a thing before a stranger, but it did not seem to faze Philip, who chuckled as they stepped out of the small inn and into the fresh air.

Sophia shivered. She had not thought to pull a pelisse around her shoulders.

Philip laughed. "Remind me—if I do find a place here, it must have plenty of fireplaces and no damp!"

They reached the door of the smithy in no time, though that was not difficult, considering the short distance between anything in that small village. It was a little unclear, however, what they were supposed to do now. Was there some sort of announcement they had to make of their presence? It was clear Angus had already started the heavier work of the day.

Sophia looked up at Philip, who shrugged. "We knock, I suppose."

He did so, and immediately the noise of hammering ceased. The door swung open and revealed a scowling man even taller than Philip. His expression changed, however, the moment he saw them.

"Newlyweds?" he grunted.

"You tell us," said Philip with a grin.

Sophia smiled. "We have a purse—a gift, for you. A token of our appreciation."

She had grabbed the leather purse as she had pulled Philip downstairs, and she was glad she had done so after the innkeeper's recommendation.

The smithy took the purse in his hand and his eyes widened. "Just how generous is this gift of yours?"

Philip blew out his cheeks. "Why, I would say—what, about twenty guineas, give or take?"

Sophia had assumed the man would be pleased with their goodwill, but he frowned. "I want no criminals in my smithy," he said slowly.

Only then Sophia realized what he had guessed—that they were on the run for some offense! Taking his hand and marveling at all those callous and burns, she smiled.

"We are no criminals, nor have any ill actions to our name," she said quietly. "All we wish is to marry and our parents—well, my parents…"

Sophia's voice trailed away. *How was she supposed to explain the absolute fanaticism that her parents had to wed her off, with bunting and frills and absolutely anyone who was anyone on the guest list?*

She glanced at Philip, who coughed and placed his left hand on her shoulder, tilting it so his signet ring was visible.

"As the Earl of Marnmouth, I would be most grateful," he said quietly. "All I wish is for a simple wedding to this young lady."

It appeared that was all the smithy needed. "Well, why did ye not say so a'fore?" Angus grinned. "Come on in."

Sophia could not help but cough as she stepped into the boiling smithy. There was the anvil, the racks of what appeared to be torture instruments, a stack of swords in one corner, a wooden bowl full of horseshoes…

"Righty, ye stand there good sir," said the smithy, pointing a finger to one side of the anvil. "And you there, miss."

Sophia took her place on the other side of the anvil.

"Now hold hands, ye ken."

Sophia reached out, and Philip took her hands in his own, clasped together over the anvil. It was hot but not unbearable, her heart still beating frantically as her whole body grew in heat and intensity.

This was it, then. This was the moment.
Her wedding.

She had avoided it for so long. She had attempted it with two others. Two gentlemen had proposed to her and decided to walk away. Now she stood with Philip Egerton, the Earl of Marnmouth. She had already given him her body and her heart, and now she would give everything else.

After all they had endured together, Philip would not walk away.

"Dearly beloved," said Angus with a grin. "We are gathered here today—"

Philip pulled his hands from hers, and Sophia's heart turned cold. *No. No, this could not be happening. Surely he could not do this to her!*

Philip wiped his hands on his coat and then clasped her hands again. "Apologies, sweet, my hands were a little moist."

Sophia attempted to slow her breathing. *It was just a coincidence.* He loved her, and she loved him. They were going to be married.

"Y'names?"

"Sophia Mariah Worsley," she said quietly. It was hard to believe that this was real. She had always believed that a wedding of hers would be in a church. But she had tried that before, and look where that had got her!

"Philip Jonathan Marnion Lewis Egerton, Earl of Marnmouth, Baronet of Cockwood."

Sophia stifled a laugh. "Really?"

Philip nodded sheepishly.

The smithy gave him a sharp look. "Really,

an earl?"

Philip sighed, and Sophia tried not to laugh. "Really, I assure you."

The man raised an eyebrow, but he said no more about it, instead saying, "Witnesses?"

Sophia bit her lip. It had not occurred to her that they would need witnesses.

"I see," said Angus with a grin. "Do not fret y'sel about it, wench, you are not the first. I can provide them, though I warn ye, they'll need gifts an' all."

Philip laughed. "Of course they will, and rightly so! Bring them in, sir, and I can procure gifts for each of them."

The smithy disappeared through a doorway, leaving Sophia and Philip holding hands over the still-hot anvil.

"Cockwood?"

"I do not want to talk about it," said Philip with a wry smile. "No second thoughts?"

Sophia smiled wryly. "No cold feet?"

Philip shook his head. "Not in this furnace."

She tightened her grip on his hands. "You know what I mean, Philip!"

His smile faded, and he looked serious as he said, "Never. I love you, Sophia. I am staying here. With you. Husband and wife, and all that."

Before Sophia could respond, Angus had returned with two women who looked as though they could be his daughters.

"Right. Witnesses," he said unnecessarily. "So, Sophia and Philip. You are bound here by the law of Scotland and the goodwill of me'sel, proprietor of this 'ere smithy, to bind your'sels together in holy matrimony."

Sophia smiled. *This was happening. This was actually going to happen.*

"Do you vow to take each other as man and wife, loving each other, being loyal 'nd true to each other, f'all the days of ye lives?"

Sophia did not look away from Philip, and he likewise kept his gaze on her as they both said, "Yes."

"Rings."

"In the purse—gift, we gave you," said Philip with a smile.

The smithy took time finding the gold rings amongst the guineas. "One each? 'Tis unusual."

"I wish to bind myself to Miss Sophia Worsley in every way possible," said Philip seriously. "That means a ring for me, too."

Sophia glowed with pleasure at his words. It was unusual, true, but it meant so much to her.

"Now, hold hands," instructed Angus. "There. Now, though you be far from home and kin, you have made new kin here today. Not only with each other, but with the village of Gretna. Ye'll always have a place 'ere, no matter where you go after I announce you, man and wife. You may kiss."

The abrupt ending surprised Sophia, laughing for joy as Philip swept around the anvil and kissed her passionately.

Their first kiss as husband and wife. Her husband.

It had all been worth it, all the heartache, to find him here at the end of her story.

After they broke apart, she could do nothing but look into his dark eyes. Her husband. *Her Philip.* She wanted nothing else but to spend the rest of her days with him.

A meaningful cough, however, reminded them they were actually in the presence of others.

"I think my witnesses may like their gifts," said Angus with a nod to his daughters.

Pulling a handful of guineas from his pocket, Philip thrust it to one of them. "Divide that between you, and thank you for your service today."

And then they were stepping out into the cold Scottish air.

She glanced at Philip and smiled. "Good morning, husband."

He grinned. "Good morning, wife. Is it time for bed yet?"

EPILOGUE

IT WAS IMPOSSIBLE to stop smiling. He did not think he ever would. *Sophia was his wife.* Sophia Worsley was not a Worsley—she was an Egerton, the Countess of Marnmouth.

But even more importantly, she was his wife.

Philip grinned as he accepted the best wishes of those surrounding him in his London Mayfair townhouse. Their words washed over him, and he barely paid any attention—why should he, when all he could do was marvel at her?

Sophia. There was no one else in the world like her, thank God, for he was quite worn out with keeping up with her. She could wear him out for the rest of his days.

"Yes, I know!" she laughed, her eyes sparkling. "And I do apologize our wedding reception is a little belated, but we simply did not think you would all travel so far north."

Philip had her arm in his and never wished to

let go. Few people wanted to speak to him; they were all focused on his bride, and he could not blame them. He was intoxicated with her mere presence.

"Yes, we were married just over a week ago—yes, at Gretna Green," she was saying to a rather disapproving Lady Romeril. "Well, we just decided we were not that interested in a wedding, and actually more interested in being married."

There were a gaggle of people around them, two of them the Lymington twins.

"My, my, your wedding sounds very dull, Miss Worsley," said Miss Isabella, if Philip was not mistaken.

Her twin sister, the far more intelligent Miss Olivia, flushed. "We are not here to critique the wedding of the *countess*, Isabella."

The first twin glanced at Sophia and then pasted a smirk across her face. "No offense meant of course, but still, you must own it is simply not right that your husband did not—"

"My dear," interrupted a gentleman.

Philip turned to see Larnwick striding toward the guests, then around them, and saw with relief the man seemed to have some sort of handle on his bride-to-be.

"My dear, please come over here and tell dear Mrs. Marnion about your wedding gown," said Larnwick with a stiff smile.

Miss Isabella Lymington preened. "The Duke

of Larnwick, you know," she informed the guests as though she was introducing him before an audience. "My intended. Of course, I certainly will—though I thought I had told dear Mrs. Marnion all about it at—"

"Now, please," said Larnwick shortly.

What glance did he exchange with his future sister-in-law—understanding or irritation? Philip could not catch it in time, but there was something interesting between them.

As the two Lymington twins and Larnwick walked away, the latter throwing Philip an apologetic look as one would over a misbehaving child, the noise around the bride started again.

"And tell us, your ladyship, what is Gretna Green like? I have heard of it, of course, but nothing can truly explain it as someone who has so recently…"

The conversation continued, but Philip did not follow it. His heart was full of Sophia, naturally, but his mind was full of Larnwick.

Poor man. He had evidently made a match for himself that would bring a small fortune, if the way Miss Isabella had shouted about her dowry was to be believed, but still. *No amount of money, surely, could make a girl like that palatable, could it?*

Still, it was difficult to feel melancholy when he was celebrating his wedding with such a creature.

A whole week. Seven days they had been man

and wife, every day better than the last. How had he managed to be this fortunate? It was a miracle he had found her. Those other gentlemen who had passed her by had been half-blind, and certainly half-mad.

It was a relief to look back now with the virtue of hindsight to see how it had all come together. After all his nonsense and hers, they found each other.

Philip smiled at the memories of their carriage journey back down to London after their hasty Gretna Green wedding. He did not think he would ever enjoy a carriage ride better than those heady hours with his new bride.

As Sophia continued to explain to all her acquaintance and friends about their experiences at Gretna Green, Philip saw his new in-laws step slowly toward him.

Releasing her arm and jerking his head to her parents, so she knew where he was going, Philip moved a little way from his bride and bowed low to Mr. and Mrs. Worsley.

"Thank you," said Mr. Worsley with no preamble, "for marrying our daughter."

Philip almost laughed. *This was ridiculous— could they not see what a jewel their daughter was?*

"The honor is absolutely all mine," he said aloud. "I cannot begin to express how fortunate I am."

The couple shared an incredulous look.

"But, your lordship—Marnmouth," said Mrs. Worsley hesitantly. "Why, you are an *earl!* You, who could have married anyone, thought to rescue from obscurity and shame our daughter who—"

"She is the best person in the world I have ever met, and I do not think I will meet better," said Philip seriously. "No number of titles will ever make me worthy of her, Mrs. Worsley. She is the better person, Mr. Worsley, and I consider myself to have landed an absolute catch."

It was clear from their expressions that he had not yet convinced them. They did not even seem to understand the concept that she could be worthy of his affections.

And perhaps, in a way, that was his own fault. He had not really done Sophia any sort of justice with his mumbling words, but it was hard to express just what Sophia meant to him.

His other soul, his second self. His better half, in all senses of the word. How could he create language that could even dream of surpassing her?

"Sophia is," he began.

"Are you singing my praises again?"

His smile broadened as Sophia approached and tucked her arm in his once more, where she belonged. "Of course!"

"Good," she said decidedly. "I expect you to do so for the rest of our lives, so 'tis excellent you are getting some practice in."

Philip saw her parents looked a little scandalized.

"Come now," said Sophia softly now and with a beseeching look at her parents. "Are you not happy for us?"

"Of course we are, child," said Mrs. Worsley with feeling. "And after everything that has happened, after past disappointments—*an earl!*"

Soon it would be as though those other engagements had never occurred, he was sure.

"I quite agree, 'tis wonderful how it has all worked out," he said aloud. "And all because of a little gamble."

Sophia nudged him in the ribs.

"Now, you must excuse me, Mama, Papa," said Philip cordially, and he saw his in-laws beam at the new names for themselves, "but I must go and check on a friend. We must. Until later."

He pulled Sophia away, and she sighed heavily as they stepped out of the drawing room and into the hallway of his townhouse. "Excellent excuse to escape my parents."

"Excuse?" said Philip quietly. "Braedon, dear man, are you quite well?"

He had spotted the gentleman a few times since they had started welcoming guests into their home for their wedding celebration, and he had looked miserable.

Now Braedon looked as though he had received bad news and was standing in the corner of the hallway, letting the revelry simply pass him by. Philip would not say he was an intimate friend of the viscount, but one did not need to know someone well to see they were unhappy.

Braedon sighed. "Yes. No, 'tis just…it does not matter, Marnmouth. Do not concern yourself about me."

His low tone only made Philip more concerned. "What has occurred?"

"Nothing, that is the trouble, it is just—oh, hang it, it does not matter," said Braedon hastily. "'Tis just an ill humor of mine, I shall snap out of it in no time."

He glanced at Sophia standing beside them, looking concerned.

"And besides, congratulations are in order!"

Sophia nodded. "Thank you, Braedon. But are you quite sure—"

"Quite sure," interrupted Braedon with a wry smile. "I am, at least."

Without another word, he wandered off into the breakfast room, which had been opened up as the swell of guests had continued.

"My word, how very odd," said Philip slowly. "I wonder what on earth is the matter with him?"

"Nothing I couldn't cure, I am sure."

Philip's heart went cold. *No, surely not. There was no chance in hell that she—*

Emma Tilbury was smiling as he turned.

"Do not concern yourself, Marnmouth, I

have not come to upend the party."

She stepped toward them, and Philip felt his stomach contract with panic. *What had she come here for?* Was this another move to demonstrate her power over him? Had they not been through that all, that strange night when he had returned, heartbroken, to London?

"Countess," said Emma as she curtseyed low to Sophia—and Philip saw in surprise Sophia repaid the compliment. "I am only in London for a little longer, I have decided to go to the Continent."

"Ah," said Philip in a half-strangle. "For the winter?"

Was that a shadow passing across her face?

"For the foreseeable future," Emma said shortly. "And before I departed this heavenly isle, I wished to give you my congratulations and best wishes for, I hope, a merry future."

Philip could hardly breathe. He had never lied to Sophia, never hidden his life from her. Had he not already arranged for them to visit his daughters? Had Sophia not already suggested that the three Egerton girls come and live with them in Marnmouth?

Children were one thing. Mistresses, even mistresses of the past, were quite another.

They had no secrets from each other, but that did not mean Sophia wished to be presented with the very physical reminder of what Philip had literally been bedding before her.

Why on earth had Emma come here?

"Yes, right, good," he said distractedly, wondering how quickly he could separate the old mistress and the new wife. "But—"

"My dear Miss Tilbury, how wonderful to see you again," said Sophia smoothly, reaching out and squeezing her hand. Philip found he was no longer breathing. "I thank you for your congratulations, and hope you enjoy your time on the Continent. The weather, I believe, will be most pleasant."

Philip forced his lungs to move, still utterly lost.

"Thank you, by the way, for your advice," Sophia continued. "It was well-timed."

Emma glanced at Philip with a wry smile before saying, "Absolutely my pleasure, Countess. Now, let me go and see if I can cheer up old Braedon."

She was gone in a rush of skirts before Philip could say anything.

Sophia was laughing. "You should see your face!"

"Wha…" Philip swallowed and tried again. "What did all that mean? What advice?"

His wife shrugged nonchalantly. "Oh, she helped me. And isn't it amazing, she did not look upset by our marriage at all."

It was impossible not to laugh. "She advised

you? The little minx, she tried to give me advice, too!"

"I thought our marriage was rebellious, but it looks like many wanted it to occur!"

"Well, I certainly did," said Philip, his heart fluttering painfully. "I have never wanted anyone more."

If she needed to hear the reassurance after that interaction with his old mistress, he had said it, but Sophia did not seem that concerned.

"So, if we have rebelled against most of society already, I think there is only one thing we can do," he quipped in a low voice.

Sophia raised a questioning eyebrow, and Philip leaned forward so he could whisper in her ear. "Let's do it again."

There was no one else in the hallway now, all the revelers further into the house, so there was no one to see him as he started to walk up the stairs, pulling his wife with him.

"Where are we going?"

Philip grinned. "Upstairs."

Sophia frowned. "What? Why? The rest of the celebration and all our friends are here. We cannot just leave!"

"I want my wife, and I'm going to have her. Celebration be damned."

He had not intended his words to be so forceful, but she was a force of nature herself.

"Ah, I see," said Sophia with a smile as they

reached the landing and slipped through into a guest bedchamber. There was a key in the door. She turned it. "But I can't be a rebel now that I'm a wife, can I?"

Philip pushed her firmly against the wall and kissed her neck. "I don't know, but I have a few ideas…"

About Emily E K Murdoch

If you love falling in love, then you've come to the right place.

I am a historian and writer and have a varied career to date: from examining medieval manuscripts to designing museum exhibitions, to working as a researcher for the BBC to working for the National Trust.

My books range from England 1050 to Texas 1848, and I can't wait for you to fall in love with my heroes and heroines!

Follow me on twitter and instagram @emilyekmurdoch, find me on facebook at facebook.com/theemilyekmurdoch, and read my blog at www.emilyekmurdoch.com.

* 9 7 8 1 9 5 3 4 5 5 5 8 1 *